STAY DEAD

BOOK ONE

STEVE WANDS

DEDICATION

Dedicated to Frank and Bob Sharkey, my uncompromising uncles, two free spirits who let me watch whatever I wanted when I came over to visit them. And to Lorraine, my grandmother, for letting me rent *Night of the Living Dead* and *Evil Dead 2,* forever damaging my brain.

CONTENTS

	Acknowledgments	viii
	Author's Note	ix
1	Dark days	1
2	Under the skies of doom	8
3	The New Haven blues	20
4	The road to Hell	30
5	Good intentions	46
6	No place like home	53
7	Blood and ash	57
8	Siege	62
9	One bad apple spoils the barrel	67
10	Can't always get what you want	70
11	The dead come slowly, but steady as the morning sun	74
12	School's out forever	80
13	Two for the road	85
14	Tomorrow never knows	90
15	Unearthed	94
16	Power to the people	104
17	One more time to kill the pain	115
18	Situation degenerates	119
19	Moths to the flame	122

20	Standing still	125
21	If it's the last thing we ever do	127
22	Runaways	129
23	Unrest	134
24	Survivors	140
25	Dead reckoning	144
26	Deeper down	158
27	Decisions	162
28	Sinking ship	172
29	And Hell followed with	176
30	Curiosity	180

STAY DEAD

ACKNOWLEDGMENTS

To my family and friends, all of which I would fight for come the end of times. To my wife and son for creating the most chaotic atmosphere in which to write. To my first readers, especially Keith Latch and Darryl L. Pierce, who helped me to shape this novel into what it is now. To Christopher Eck, for answering all of my questions regarding power outages. To Rick Galer for reading the novel and emailing me several mistakes and notes afterwards to make the book better. To Adam Staffaroni for some much needed editing. Thank you all.

AUTHOR'S NOTE

This novel takes place in a fictionalized version of our world. We spend a lot of time in New Jersey and West Virginia but they are not quite the states as you know them. Any resemblance to actual incidents, or to any person living or dead, is purely coincidental.

STEVE WANDS

Thus that which is the most awful of evils, death, is nothing to us, since when we exist there is no death, and when there is death we do not exist.

—Epicurus

1 DARK DAYS

The world didn't end overnight.

Peoria, Illinois. The United States of America.
On the news set at Channel 5, KPIL a sultry woman with jet-black hair and olive skin cocks her head and smiles at the camera. She sits next to a handsome man in his mid thirties. While waiting for the commercial break to end, she and her co-anchor are making jovial small talk with one another. They share the same plastic smile, perfect teeth and flawlessly coiffed hair, but off air they share nothing but contempt for one another. In their ear-pieces the co-anchors hear "We are back in three," they end their chuckling and stiffen up, "Two," for the next segment, "One!" The woman shuffles her papers, cocks her head and smiles at the camera.

"A woman who had been pronounced dead at her home by a doctor was found to be alive in a hospital morgue when a family friend there to identify the presumed deceased saw that she seemed to be breathing. The woman then began moving and attacked the family friend. Witnesses said she was belligerent and unintelligible," the anchorwoman smiled at the camera.

"That is one crazy story, Lorelei. We hope the woman is in better health and out of the morgue," her smarmy coworker chuckled then went on.

Japan.

Prisons across Japan have been executing mentally ill inmates, which is a clear violation of U.N. standards for individuals suffering from mental illness. Despite numerous accounts documenting the issue, Japan's Justice Ministry official, Akiro Ishi, has denied all accusations.

Prisoners given the death penalty are kept in solitary confinement, sometimes for decades, and are not told when their sentence is to be carried out until the morning of their execution. This method can lead to "significant mental illness," a London-based human rights group reported.

The group created major headline news but was unable to gain any ground on the situation. They, along with U.N. officials, were denied access to any prisoners on death row. Japanese officials were quoted as saying, "…a death sentence means death…mental illness is not a reprieve from punishment."

What the report and subsequent articles failed to mention was that moments after execution the bodies of the executed returned to life. The families of the executed have yet to bury their dead.

Kunduz, Afghanistan.
Sean Ferral, a British Journalist reporting on the aftermath of a NATO air strike when he and his interpreter were abducted. Seventy people including some women and children died as a result of the air strike. Special Forces raided the bunker in which Ferral and his interpreter were kept—though neither of them survived the raid. The Department of Defense refused to comment.

Unreported was the fierce hand-to-hand battle fought between the Special Forces and the reanimated airstrike victims that resulted in four U.S. soldiers killed in action and three more missing.

Lacy, California. The United States of America.
The body of an 8-year-old girl, Sandra Binantu, was found stuffed inside of a suitcase in a pond near her home. Her Sunday school teacher, 28-year-old Melissa Chuckaby, who is also the mother of one of Sandra's closest playmates, has been accused of her murder.

Sandra's family has been denied access to the body and has been instructed by federal authorities to "not make any funeral arrangements at this time."

The authorities did not tell her parents that the body of Sandra Binantu could not be found after she was reported to have walked out of the county morgue.

Istanbul, Turkey.
A fatal flash flood roared through a valley near the city, and at least 300 people have gone missing. In a news conference at Istanbul's Disaster Management Center, Turkey's prime minister, called the floods the worst disaster of the century. The prime minister blamed the high death toll on record rainfall and on developers, who have constructed buildings in vulnerable riverbeds and known flood plains. The Disaster Management Center is in the process of searching for the bodies.

The Prime Minister neglected to report that they had lost contact with the first two rescue teams sent to the area.

Sydney, Australia.
Researchers have begun testing the H1N1 vaccine for contaminants after massive reports of side effects, and, in some cases, death. After 19 days, blood samples showed that most participants stayed or became even more susceptible to the virus and in addition had developed long lasting side effects including paralysis, heart palpitations, and even death. There are reports of victims lapsing into coma then recovering and attacking hospital staff. Researchers are baffled. The Center for Disease Control has issued a warning against taking the vaccine and is in the process of recalling all H1N1 vaccines. Vaccine related deaths continue to climb.

Across the world, the dead walk.
Many nations of the world have declared martial law, and the United Nations has declared a state of emergency throughout the world.

Many believed it was the end of times.

***

The incessant beep-beep-beep of the alarm clock jolted Scott from a warm and comfortable nook he managed to squirm into during the night. He was nuzzled up between his wife and their aging cat, Steamer. Judy, his wife, calls him Mister Butters, as it was the original name they had agreed upon. Scott, had recently begun to call him Steamer, and on special occasions he'd been given the moniker of Sir Farts-a-Lot. Scott begrudgingly rose out of bed, rubbing the glasslike crust from the corners of his eyes and straightening out his shorts, which somehow managed to nearly twist around his lower half. He blindly fingered for the off switch and eventually found it, putting an end to the beep-beep-beep machine till it would go off again tomorrow morning and the two of them would once again square off like a couple of gunslingers in the old west. Steamer stretched slowly at the corner of the bed, eyeing up Scott as he pulled a plain white T-shirt over his head and exited the room. Once Scott was out of sight, Steamer lay down in the empty warm nook next to Judy and proceeded to earn his special occasions nickname.

Judy buried her head under the pillow as she muttered, "Jesus, Scott, thanks a lot!"

Scott walked into the kitchen and turned on the laptop computer that sat on top of a heap of business papers that neither he nor Judy could force themselves to do last night. Among them were three obituaries that needed to be sent to the local newspapers by 11:00 am today, concerning the three houseguests they had on tables downstairs in the basement mortuary. He walked over to the pantry and grabbed a coffee filter while trying to decide what flavor of which brand he felt like having. After little debate he grabbed the half-empty pouch of New England's Eye-Opener Blend, and began heaping spoonfuls into the filter. By the time it began brewing he was already opening up his web browser to read the morning news. He wasn't surprised at the headline, but scoffed regardless. THE DEAD RISE, in big bold capital letters. For days there had been random reports and articles popping up in print, online, radio, and television with regards to eye witness accounts of the dead returning to life. Scott dealt with death on a daily basis. He was born into a business of death, and if anyone knew anything about the dead it was he. And he had yet to see one get up and walk out of his home.

He was convinced it was the major media outlets' way of cashing in on the popularity of zombie movies in the last few months. It seemed like a new one hit movie screens once a month, and Scott didn't see the appeal—they weren't the slightest bit realistic. A dead body almost immediately begins to enter into rigor mortis, which would make walking, let alone running nearly impossible. He found the entire idea laughable; yet there it was in big bold capital letters which meant it had to be true.

He read past the title, just out of curiosity, looking at the images, and the links to video clips. After reading the article he came to the conclusion that he found it interesting, and very entertaining. He wanted more. Scott loved a good read. He had a whole room dedicated to reading—it was full of books. Many of them were instructional and pertaining to his craft, but many more were science fiction, fantasy, and even a few horror books. Though if you were to ask him if he read horror books he would tell you no.

Below the article were links to similar stories. He clicked on the next one. He could hear the coffee maker gurgling to a finish, and turned just in time to see the green light go on. He fetched a cup from the cupboard. The cup read "I like it hot". He filled it to the brim and drank it black and bitter, as he returned to his laptop. He read the next article, and then the next one after that. He visited other sites, and eventually turned on the television—the news of the dead not dying was everywhere. He fetched another cup of coffee and sipped it as he stared blankly at the television. He was almost convinced the dead really were upright and mobile again.

Judy stumbled downstairs, scratching just below the waistline of her silky black shorts with Mister Butters following just behind her. She filled up a cup of her own and walked around to Scott's backside. She patted her wild hair down, trying to tame it and look appealing. She hoped that maybe they could get a quick morning screw in before the day swept them away and left them too tired to do anything but sleep when it was over. She leaned over and was about to kiss his neck when she noticed the television. She sat down next to him with the same blank expression. The two skeptics sat there trying to decipher if the news was real or not. If it was on television, it had to be real, but it couldn't be.

"Don't you think if the dead were really coming back to life, we'd be among the first to know?"

"You would think."

"How did you sleep last night?"

"Slept like a brick. I feel a little raw today, though."

"Well, if it's end of the world, maybe we should go back upstairs and get under the covers."

"I need some coffee first. You did keep me up late last night."

"I couldn't sleep, and it didn't sound like you were complaining."

"Pretty sure I yelled 'no'."

"Sure that wasn't 'oh'?"

They polished off the pot of coffee while they watched the presidential address from an undisclosed location. The president read his notes calmly, as if he'd been practicing for days but his face had a subtle expression of hidden horror, which could only be conveyed by the best actors or the truest reactions.

They stared at the television, as if in a trance, then a noise came from downstairs. They turned to each other, the trance broken, fearful yet disbelieving as they stood up. What was downstairs would surely be the deciding factor between fact and fiction.

Leaving their unfinished coffee behind, they headed downstairs. They passed the two large visitation rooms and the formal office for bereaved customer consultations. They passed a closet where they kept the embalming chemicals, and then stood quietly at the next door. They listened for a moment. Hearing nothing Scott opened the door, turned on the light and led the way to the basement.

The area was bright and open, two stainless steel tables stood at the center of the room, surrounded by cabinetry full of chemicals and equipment used to prepare the bodies of the dead for their eternal rest. They didn't have a crematorium on the premises but Scott was hopeful that in the next three years they'd be able to afford one and the accompanying expansion to house it. To the right of the tables was a walk in refrigerator where the dead were stored. It was closed, and that's exactly how they both remembered leaving it.

As they stepped closer they could hear a thumping noise. It was a gentle noise, but one that repeated itself. As they stepped closer it became more erratic and forceful.

Scott paused, looking back to the steps, but since Judy stepped forward he had to as well. They now stood at the door, ready to open it. Scott stood near the lip of the door with his heart beating wildly and his mind filling with childlike wonder. Judy held the handle and readied herself to open it. Scott gave her the nod to open it, and she did.

2 UNDER THE SKIES OF DOOM

It was a warm night. Bugs flitted through the air and chirped in the tall grass surrounding the campsite. The trees lurched upward to the pinpricked backdrop of the evening sky, like rockets bound for space. And if they were capable of it they'd be foolish not to go. A ragtag group of individuals had only stopped to rest in the sanctuary of the woodland retreat for a few hours, come morning they would continue toward Titan City to find their families, friends, and loved ones. The woods were filled with more than the usual creatures that night. The living dead haunted the earth, even in the most serene of locations.

A young man sat by the wheel well of his car scribbling notes, and thoughts into a warped notepad. His eyes looked tiny, dry, and bloodshot. His stubble was transforming into a beard and when he couldn't think of something to write he scratched at his stubble with the eraser side of the pencil.

"Look at this fucking guy," says Frankie. "Snap out of it! You're not turning into a zombie on me are you?"

"Huh? Heh, no, not yet you bearded bastard. I hope you got another one of those Bud's for me," said Eddie, closing his notebook, the pencil holding the page.

"For you? Hell no, not on me at least, there's a cooler behind the passenger seat. We'll have to make a run later and pick up some more," Frankie almost looked happy about it.

"Shit, there's never gonna be enough. I'm sure we're minutes away from the last cold beer on earth, but…fuck it, it's not like we've never had warm, skunky beer before," Eddie said.

"Well, now we don't have to worry about the cops breaking it up and pissing on the fire," Frankie replied, even though they were both of age now.

They turned to look at the growing pile of burning bodies, it seemed like they would always have fire. Whether they were in the woods, or on the road the dead had a way of finding them. Luckily, they had gotten good at protecting themselves and dispatching the dead things that sought their flesh. Not everybody was keen on burning the bodies. They all had reasons, and some of them good, but in the end majority rules and majority ruled that the dead sons and daughters of bitches and bastards would burn as bright as the stars in the sky, and that was that.

On their way back to Frankie's truck neither one of them could help staring at the blank faces of the people with whom they traveled. It seemed they were all on a road to nowhere. Some of the early survivors had figured out how to put the dead things down for good. Eventually the television news media picked up on it and shared the information before they went off the air more or less permanently. Destroy the brain, remove the head, or burn the body had become known as the surefire bets. One bullet was usually insufficient to dispatch the creatures. A shotgun blast, or a high caliber hunting rifle could do the trick if used properly. Most of the survivors used baseball bats, crowbars and the like when it came to one-on-one combat with the dead. It allowed them to conserve ammunition and create less noise. It was also easier to brain the creatures than it was to make headshots. Most of the time when it came to this sort of combat it was to escape death rather than deal it—so, of course the damage wasn't sufficient to keep them down. The dead had made a habit of coming back.

Once seated on the back of Frankie's black, beat-to-hell Dodge Ram Eddie managed to take only one swig of his not-quite-cold brew before old man Ricker came lurking around.

"Anybody making a run tonight?" He asked, biting on his dirty fingernails.

Almost afraid to answer, Frankie said, "not sure, nobody's been talking much today."

"That blows, I sure could use some more smokes…" as if nobody knew what he wanted when he came over in the first place. "Any of you boys got one?" he continued.

"C'mon Ricker, you know neither of us smoke just like we know you don't drink…yet." Eddie chimed in. He was halfway done with his Budweiser, trying to savor it but not really being able to.

"Ricker, you fucking leech, I got one," shouted Dawn. Dawn was a chain-smoking waitress with a mouth like all the other chain-smoking waitresses that had worked at Pete's Pit Stop Diner on Route 9.

Ricker made his way over to her with one hand out and the other fishing for a light in his pocket, but there wasn't one there. He was convinced his fingers were lying and that one of them would eventually come clean. She knew he didn't have a light, so she used the lit end from the smoke that had been hanging from her pinkish-orange lips and lit it for him. When she gave it to him it had her colors around the end of it. Either not seeing the lipstick or not caring, he put it between his lips and puffed away. He nodded his head in thanks, looking her over as he did; she wasn't bad looking…so long as she didn't talk much. Ricker hated women who talked too much.

Eddie cracked open another beer, his pace just behind Frankie's, making sure he didn't jump ahead on his pal's stash. He had just swallowed his first swig when the dead things crept up on the group. There weren't many of them, but it was never good to be caught off guard by dead things that wanted to eat your skin, no matter how few. It looked as if most of them were kids, scouts by their uniforms. Out for a retreat at one of the campgrounds, one from which they hadn't returned.

From behind Eddie and Frankie charged Gerty. Gerty, short for Gertrude, was brandishing a very well used Louisville Slugger baseball bat. She felt no remorse as she bashed in the first child's head. She was a brute of a human, let alone a woman. Frankie jumped to his feet and pulled his shotgun from behind the passenger's seat. Eddie grabbed a bat from the bed of the truck.

The three of them took care of the small group of scouts. Their scout leader staggered out from the woods alongside another gentleman, clearly older, and another youngster. Gerty turned to swing, knocking the older man off to the side. Frankie blasted his face clear off, getting gristle and chunks of grey matter all over his shirt and arms as the noise of the shotgun blast echoed through the woods. Gerty kept swinging. Eddie was batting clean up with a splintered bat that had gore dripping from it. The three of them had the same look of intensity in their eyes. The same look of thirst, blood thirst. Eddie knocked the last youngster's jaw into oblivion, screaming like some wild savage. He continued bashing the freckle-faced Cub Scout into the dirt, smashing his face into a puddle of dark red mush. The savage pounding pulled noises from the child's body that contrasted with the thudding of the wooden fury. The sounds made those who watched gag, and as was inevitable, someone puked.

Someone always does.

This time it was Eddie's slightly younger brother, Joseph, who, hours earlier, was doing the same thing to a man old enough to be his father. It wasn't easy for any of them to kill, but with each passing day the difficulty diminished. They did it because they had to. The smart ones lost themselves in the necessity of the action and were able to pull themselves out when it was over.

The vicious attack ran its course and everyone walked away. Scott and Judy came up to drag the bodies to the burn pile. They both used what looked like ice picks of some sort, hooking the bodies just under the ribs. They did it as if they had always done it. The killing three walked back to where they had been before the violent scene, in an odd state of utter disgust and acceptance of what they had just been capable of doing. None of them cared to wipe the blood or gore off, though they probably should have. It was as if they temporarily shut down.

Joseph went up to his brother and put his hand firmly on his shoulder. He looked at him with an exhausted stare. It had never felt so strange to him as it did now. He felt like he was looking behind a plate of streaked glass.

The night carried on, it was quiet and the stars were bright. There were no electrical hums, no cars beeping, no stupid cell phone jingles—only the crackling and blistering of dead flesh. It smelled horrendous, but everyone seemed to be getting used to it, especially Scott and Judy, who were roasting marshmallows. Most of the group thought them to be sick in the head. Almost everyone had heard the Cliff Notes version of their story; husband and wife, ran a funeral home in North Amber and had dead bodies year round in the home they slept in. Scott supposedly had eaten off of a plate sitting on the chest of a cadaver that happened to be delivered during his mealtime. If you were to ask him about it he'd have a different take on the story every time.

Some of the group started falling asleep, mostly the younger kids who were exhausted and scared out of their minds. Not that everyone else was taking the new world order in stride. Everyone was scared to hell, but you couldn't survive like that; some people had to step up and the lead the way, while others simply followed. Luckily for this group, many of the folks had stepped up. They had a few good people who helped keep everyone safe. Boone, who was practically running the show, Gerty, Eddie, Frankie, Alexis, Jon-Jon, and Big Cups were all doing their best to get them to Titan City. They did more than they had to. That was how they handled the new reality, by keeping busy and finding something to do and someone to help.

Titan City seemed like a world away. It was everything they needed it to be. It was a destination, it was hope, and it was the green grass on the other side of hell that surely had to be better than the grass they were standing on now.

They were almost out of Middlesex County, near rural towns like Sheffield, Perch, and New Haven. They had intended to be out of Middlesex County yesterday and find a place that would put some solid walls around them so they could safely rest. They needed rest something fierce. Good rest, not the sleeping on the road kind of rest that they had been getting. The campgrounds were a step in the right direction but it had still been hell on them. The woods had been both a blessing and curse, not being seen was great but not being able to see what lurked in the darkness of the brush was dangerous.

Everyone old enough took turns keeping watch while others slept. It was only fair to share the responsibilities of keeping the group safe. Along with traveling they had raided strip malls, convenience stores, and gas stations to get what they needed and be on their way. They did their best to stay off the main streets and highways, which, could be dangerous and impassable. But every road held a hidden danger.

Jon-Jon groggily climbed out of his van. It was an old blue Chevrolet Astro Van with rust spreading out from its wheel wells. It had dents and dings on all sides. The front grill was spattered with blood and chunks of skin. Jon-Jon wore a trucker cap, maroon with piss-yellow letters that spelled out "Milf Hunter". It was the kind of hat that nobody else could have gotten away with wearing, but he did. He also sported a brown vest over a two-day old flannel shirt he snatched on the last raid, although it could've just as easily been something hanging in his closet.

"Does anyone have any fuckin' toilet paper," he stated more than asked. He waited a moment, took off his hat and scratched his forehead, put it back on and closed his eyes. "None of you fuckers got--"

Before he could finish his next few words Gerty rifled a four pack of Angel Soft at the back of his head. "Quit yer yelling faggot! Pop-a-squat and let's raid that Mal-Mart we passed on the way here."

"Yeah, yeah," he said, picking up the bucket on the side of his truck. "If you hear me screaming I may need help wiping my ass, so hurry over."

"If that's the case, you're fucked, don't be too long. I'll round up some of these other faggots," then continued to tie up her shit kickers and put on her finest insulated flannel which was a hell of a lot older than two days.

By the time Jon-Jon got back with his empty bucket and upset expression, the group had been rounded: Eddie, Joseph, Frankie, Dawn, Big Cups and of course Gerty. No one in the group was put off by the thought of going out on a raid. To them it had become fun, dangerous—certainly, but an adventurous necessity to cling to their old way of living and their new way of survival. What they had experienced fleeing their homes were the things of nightmares. Running into a few lurkers while on a raid was expected and worth the risk for the things they needed (even though most of the stuff they had been taking wasn't out of need). It was out of habit, desire, and plainly because they could.

Big Cups was on walkie-talkie duty for the group, and it was Joseph's turn to scout for batteries, bandages, and aspirins. Frankie had been given the pleasure of looking out for new wheels. Dawn had to get a new outfit because her diner uniform just wasn't cutting it anymore: It was torn up and stunk to high hell, and everyone could certainly agree on that. The rest were just along for the ride.

They all hopped into the back of Frankie's truck. He drove and Joseph rode shotgun, ironic now because there actually was a shotgun behind the seat. They had their guns, bats, knives, and gloves. They noticed nothing on their trek, not so much as an abandoned car. The streetlights were still on; Joseph wondered if there was a group of diehard JPG Electric & Company employees keeping it running. Frankie's truck was running low on fuel. They had slightly more than an eighth of a tank. Someone would be getting the honorable duty of siphoning out an abandoned luxury SUV, or, if luck should have, a larger vehicle.

Finally, they reached their destination. The truck, barely at a snail's pace, rounded the outer rim of the parking lot. They scouted for lurkers, survivors, or anything that could complicate things before committing to the raid. It was clear except for a few cars, some shopping carts, and two bodies that were not getting back up. They drove around the building, getting in closer with each sweep, like a vulture circling its prey. Around back were a few shipping trucks. The docks were vacant except for one truck backed in to a loading bay. The garbage containers were waiting for a garbage truck that would never show up. There were pallet stacks and a lonely little power jack next to a wall full of milk crates. They took one final lap and ended up right in front of the main doors.

The doors were locked up with a chain on the outside; the glass was spider webbed from top to bottom. Beyond the initial doors was a smaller area filled with vending machines, quarter eaters, and tiny benches. Not much more was visible from where they stood. Gerty grabbed a crow bar from the bed of the truck. She popped the chain.

From inside the heart of the consumer's discount paradise came the moans of dead things. They were on an all night shopping spree, looking for the last bits of warm flesh. It was a sound the raiders knew all too well. They could tell there were a lot more of them than they had bullets, bats, and hands to hold them. It was time to step back from the door and work in reverse.

Frankie headed to the left side of the parking lot to check out a vehicle he spotted when they pulled in. Joseph grabbed the gas container from the bed of the truck and picked out the closest SUV (they usually had plenty of fuel to share). Dawn followed him, siphoning was a two-man job: one to siphon and one to act as lookout. Dawn took the job with ease, it would give her time to take a few puffs, which wasn't the best idea, but Joseph didn't really mind.

Eddie hung around the door, keeping an eye on the dead things. Gerty was keeping him company. Jon-Jon looked like he was going to cry; the poor bastard hadn't been able to shit right since this would-be-apocalypse started. Big Cups was just plain nervous. He was biting his nails and scratching his crotch. He skittered over to Dawn and they split a cigarette. Having his shaky hands taking and passing a lit cigarette while Joseph was siphoning gasoline was a terrible idea. Joseph was thankful that he'd filled his canister as Cups was pulling his first drag.

Frankie's first choice of a new set of wheels didn't pan out, but he eventually found a decent station wagon—it had room for six and plenty of storage with a roof rack. The gas tank was nearly full and the tires looked to be in great shape. He drove it up alongside his Dodge. He was almost embarrassed to see the two of them next to each other, like his truck had feelings. Regardless, Frankie was loyal to his Dodge and he would stick with it till one of them died.

Everything outside was set. The Dodge had been refueled and the gas can was full. They had a new set of wheels for their traveling band, and were prepared to venture inside. Big Cups would stay behind with a walkie-talkie and a .38 special Smith & Wesson handgun. His nerves were as taut as a rubber band stretched to its limit. Though he went on every raid, he could never muster the fortitude to go into any of the stores they raided. His duty was to guard the door and make sure there were no surprises coming or going, and that was about all he could handle.

The group kept all walkie-talkie communication to a minimum. Less noise in these situations was for the best. Once the deaders spread out the group entered the store. As they passed through the main doors, they noticed the secondary doors were locked too. Gerty looked around and spotting the lurkers inside, she planned accordingly. She then broke the lock, and the raiders were in. A few lurkers were close by and turned toward the noise. Or perhaps it was the scent of fresh meat on the sales floor, no one could be certain. They weren't sure how the deaders knew when a living person was around, and most of the time they didn't care, but now they'd rather not find out. The lurkers moaned and raised their arms to the best of their inability and lurched forward. These few would be a breeze;

they were in bad repair, and slower than the freshly dead.

Gerty used the crowbar she already had handy. Hollering like a cowboy she began her battering of one of the lurker's head. It caved in with one bash, like a soggy pumpkin slamming against the street. Its blood didn't gush out. It was coagulated and dripped slowly from the gaping hole. The dead shopper dropped to the ground. Just to be safe, she continued to pulverize the dead man's head. His brains and skull looked like a finger-painting on the white tiled floor. By the time she finished, the remaining lurkers had been taken care of by her companions.

Frankie was approaching another small group of dead things while Dawn was drawn to the first sales bin they'd come across. The bin was full of cheap make-up and discounted DVD's. An odd tie-in, but there it was nonetheless. Frankie savagely attacked the next pair of flesh eaters. The blood flowed toward a battery display that Frankie didn't see at first. It was nearly empty. He called Joseph over and then Frankie threw the batteries into his backpack. Moans echoed throughout the building but the lurkers remained out of view.

Standing in front of the men's section, which was nearly bare, like the rest of store, was a rack with belts and a few fanny packs. Everybody but Eddie grabbed as many as they could. Eddie stepped over to the sock and underwear racks instead. Once the others saw them, they did the same. Frankie grabbed some thermals, hats, and gloves. The bags they carried were already swelling up. Frankie and Joseph headed back to Big Cups and tossed him the full bags. As they headed back toward the others, a lurker reached out from behind a display and grabbed Joseph by his shirt. Joseph dropped to the floor and Frankie mashed its face in. Joseph kicked at the creature, a woman who must have worked there. She was wearing a green vest with a 'can I help you' button on it. Frankie gave her one last whack to the side of her head. She was a small woman, possibly even attractive at one point, but now her deep blue eyes were a paste under Frankie's shoe.

"Spill in aisle 9," Joseph said with a smile.

Joseph got up and turned around to hear the others engaged in their own blood sport. The two of them took off in a hurry to join the others. There were at least fifteen creatures clawing at their friends. It was a scary situation in a tight spot, so they had to act fast and carefully. There wasn't room for everybody to be swinging away with abandon.

Frankie cocked his tarnished, scratched, and bloodied shotgun and shredded two lurkers a safe distance from the others. The shotgun's roar echoed through the store, and left cotton in his ears. He would have preferred to use it as a bludgeon, loud noise usually brought more trouble than it was worth, but he needed a fast solution to the problem. One of the two lurkers needed to be finished off, its head was left dangling by threads of flesh and brittle bone, its blood ran like thick dark mud. Gerty swung her crowbar and lifted it into the air, spewing muddy blood as it arched toward the bag section. What had been fifteen were quickly reduced to less than a dozen. With the help of Eddie and Frankie, they were able to put the remaining dead things down for good.

Then, a gunshot echoed through the store. The gang stopped moving and stood staring at each other. It did not come from one of them.

"Where'd that come from?" Joseph asked.

"Don't know, let's check on Cups," Gerty said in a raspy out of breath voice.

They ran toward the entrance, Big Cups stood up and asked, "What's going on in there? Are we getting out of here?"

"Not yet, we heard a shot and it wasn't one of ours, we came to check..."

"Guess that means someone's in there with a gun or...one of those fucks has one," Eddie cut her off, "either way, I'm going back in."

Eddie ran back to where they were just a moment earlier. The others followed right behind him, everybody looking in a different direction. Another shot echoed overhead, resonating in the high ceiling, curious brows were raised. Another, then another, they ran toward the noise, which brought them to a set of warehouse doors. The doors had bloody streaks and windows about the size of a shoebox. The windows were too bloody to see through. Hearts raced furiously. Frankie came forward and kicked the door open and revealed a loading bay full of lurkers.

The dead things turned, and though no dead things had ever expressed any visible emotions, they almost looked pissed. One had eyes so damaged they were completely red. They must've been truckers, vendors, or employees. They appeared fresher than the others that were in the store, cleaner, quicker. More shots fired from somewhere behind these creatures. The dead things moved toward the party crashers, as Frankie blasted them with his Remington 870 shotgun. He popped as many shots off as he could, and whoever was behind the creatures was using theirs as well. The deaders came forward. Dawn took off running and Jon-Jon followed behind. Gerty took off too and grabbed Eddie, pushing him to follow her. These deaders were quick and the area to fight them in was tight.

Eddie shouted to Joseph and Frankie, "Let's go, come on!"

Someone was still shooting from within the warehouse. The sound seemed to follow them as they made their way to the check out lanes. The lurkers were not far behind. They were clumsy and stiff but managed to keep close. Frankie reloaded. One of the more limber of the lurkers was crossing through the checkout lane, its stiff arms and hands outstretched in a hunger-driven grasp. Frankie pumped his Remington and raised it just in time to blast the lunging bastard in the mouth. Tooth, brain, both of its eyeballs and thick dark blood rained from its head and neck. Frankie continued to level the creatures that stumbled toward him and his friends. Bodies started piling up in front of the lanes. Gunshots were still getting closer. The creatures were severely thinned at this point. Gerty, Eddie, Joseph, and Jon-Jon were able to finish off the creatures. The store was quiet.

"Hello?" Eddie called.

No answer. Eddie tried again.

"Hello? We're just here for some supplies, we don't want any trouble."

Still the place was quiet.

"Hello back at ya," a man stepped into view. He was holding a Glock. "Not so fast, please, let's keep it simple." The man raised his other hand in a gentle fashion, "I'm Ben. I got some pals in the warehouse. We're just here for some supplies then we're getting back on the road too."

The man lowered his gun and headed back to the warehouse. They followed Ben, eager to see some other people. Gerty engaged the man in conversation. She had a bad feeling about him. There was something in his eyes that reminded her of her father and something instinctual that scratched at her heart. A conversation could go a long way to reveal a person, at least in her experiences they had. The words were never as telling as the expressions, and nothing was more revealing than the eyes.

The others began grabbing items and bagging them. Passing the woman's department, Dawn pulled over to the side and Jon-Jon watched her back. She quickly stripped off her clothes and started putting new stuff on. She moved ferociously, as any woman would do had they been allowed to shop for free. She grabbed enough clothes to wear a new outfit everyday of the week, and then decided she needed more. After picking up panties, bras, and socks, she had two backpacks full. They needed to go back and dump them into the truck.

The others continued on to the warehouse. Jon-Jon and Dawn headed out toward Cups, grabbing anything and everything, magazines, candy bars, trading cards. Big Cups looked at them like a homeless kitten. Jon-Jon smiled and tossed him a package of Reese's Big Cups. His grin took up the lower half of his face. On the way back in, Jon-Jon asked Dawn to guard the door to the men's room. Jon-Jon went in slowly inspecting every stall before committing, the first one had shit all over the seat, the second wasn't too bad, but wasn't keeping much of the scent out. The third stall was a charmer, a little piss on the seat, but to him this was luxury seating. He smiled as he cleaned off the seat with a wad of toilet paper. He plopped down and picked up one of those celebrity news magazines off the floor. He wiped his ass and washed his hands. The bathroom was fairly clean considering it was the end of the world. The soap was still pink and the paper towels were plentiful. Amazing, he thought, fucking amazing.

3 THE NEW HAVEN BLUES

Days earlier...

The radio was playing loudly on Jeff's porch. He and his father, Walter, were carrying planks of wood back and forth from the shed to the house. Walter and his family decided that they weren't going to leave town. They would board up his son's home, and hold out until this thing blew over. The radio, WNJOA 101.9 to be exact, kept telling them to get to a safe zone, but they were not about to take orders from anyone.

Most of the people in New Haven took off days ago in a hurry after the initial reports hit the air. A few other families in town were going to stick it out as well. Gupp's Hardware had stayed open days after any other store had dared to.

Walter pulled a bandana from his back pocket and wiped his forehead. He couldn't believe how much he was sweating. Walter was always the last to sweat. He wondered if it was old age setting in or his nerves, he hoped neither. Jeff took off his hat, wiped his brow and put it back on. Then he looked at his watch.

"The news should've come on by now," Jeff said to his father.

"Well, they're still playing the Beatles, how bad could it be?" His father said with a halfhearted smile.

"Guess we'll find out," Jeff said, picking up a big sheet of plywood.

They had most of the house boarded up. The upstairs windows were left alone except the two windows near the big tree, neither Jeff, or his father wanted to risk having those things climbing in. Jeff thought it would be a good idea to gather all the alcohol upstairs in case they needed to make Molotov's, and throw them from the upstairs windows. Walter agreed. He also thought it was a good idea to come up with an escape plan should they need to leave in a hurry. They had the family van stocked up and ready to go near the side of the house. Inside the van Jeff placed a map, water, food, clothes, and even a blanket.

Walter's spouse, Laura had been in the kitchen making lunch for everyone. She wanted to use up what food she could without having it go to waste. The town lost power two days ago and the freezer was as cold as tepid water. The food would go bad soon without the electricity. There was also a big freezer in the basement and it hadn't been opened since the power went out. They hoped to keep the food cold inside for as long as possible. Laura hoped the power would be back on before they would have to deal with that problem, which was tiny when compared to the problem of the walking dead, but still one that warranted attention.

Jeff's wife, Maria, had done major shopping before the state of emergency was declared. Their family was a large one. Jeff and Maria Caulfield had three children; Little Wally, Sandra, and Tommy. Jeff also had a sister, Barbara, who was staying with them as was his parents. She planned for the extra company and got as much food as she could afford. The house was large enough to accommodate them all, and larger than their own. It was also a bit more isolated. They had a radio with plenty of batteries, and two old lanterns from when Walter would take them camping. They had plenty of candles, and a fireplace, which they planned to light soon. It was starting to get chilly, which was odd for this time of year, and dark.

"Lunch is ready!" Laura yelled out the door, not knowing they were only a few feet away.

"What took you so long ma? I'm starving," Jeff said sarcastically but meant every word.

"Has the news come on yet?" She asked, looking downright depressed.

"Not yet. They're still playing music though, so I'm sure it'll be on soon enough," Walter tried to reassure her, but wasn't all too sure of it himself.

They gathered in the family room. It was a large room with two couches, a coffee table, and a framed painting of a shed in the woods that would've impressed Bob Ross himself. There were plants on end tables, an entertainment center that wasn't entertaining anyone, and a boarded up window that allowed almost no light inside.

Laura lit the fireplace.

***

What remained of the New Haven Police department had gathered at Mourningside Cemetery. News reports never stated anything about the buried dead coming back to life and digging their way out, but they weren't taking any chances. The police gathered friends and pretty much anyone else with a gun to survey the area. It wasn't a large cemetery, but it was big enough. It was the town's only cemetery and if you weren't catholic you were buried somewhere else outside of town. They walked in rows, following the rigid grid set forth by the headstones like a search party. They checked for unearthed caskets, or any sign of something trying to come up from the ground. They moved slowly, working their way towards the mausoleums at the rear of the cemetery. There were no recent deaths in town, the last one occurred a month ago; underage kids in a drunk driving accident. They were leaving a school football game and hit a pole doing 75 miles an hour. The car was ripped in half and so were the four kids in the car. Three had been buried toward the back, the fourth was a Jewish girl buried in the town over. She and her boyfriend weren't even drinking. According to everyone who knew them they were a couple of upstanding kids. A truer tragedy had never occurred, so whispered the lips of those who knew of them. Those who really knew them, though, knew they loved to walk around in a heroin haze and that they sucked dick for China White— the good shit. After just over an hour they had checked every inch of ground but the six mausoleums. The large group gathered near the first one.

"Keith, Alan, and Henry, get up here, now," shouted Sheriff Bruce Davis.

Alan replied, "sure thing, boss man. But you're going in first."

"That's fine with me, you big pussy. Everybody, listen up. If nothing's moving we lock it up and get the fuck out of here" Davis shouted.

At the edge of town near the North roadblock, the sky grows dim. Fires burn in the distant city and smoke chokes the light out of the day. There are only three police cruisers and six officers at the North Roadblock. No one is permitted into town without clearance from the Sheriff. There hasn't been any noise on the ham, and nothing worthwhile on the radio. A car drives up from behind the roadblock: it's Susan Kemp. Susan owns the corner deli on Main Street, appropriately named Main Street Deli. She parked off to the side of the road and got out, holding three thermoses full of coffee.

Officer Dane Kelly walked over to her. They had been together for the last few years. Both were divorced, Dane's was a messy one while Susan's was mutual. Her husband became very distant and as a result she looked at their relationship and came to the conclusion that they should have never been married to begin with. Susan met Dane, they made each other laugh and that was that. They weren't up each other's asses, and both having gone through one marriage had no intentions of suffering another. One thing led to another and now she was bringing him coffee, it was a love like so many others.

"Brought you and the boys some coffee. This one's French vanilla, the other two are regular. I brought some powdered creamer and sugar. No milk though," she said, her brownish red hair blowing in the wind.

"You are awesome. The boys will love anything at this point, but I'm taking the French vanilla for myself," Dane said as he put his hand on her hip.

"When are you getting off?" she asked. They were staying at her place, and still trying to figure out what to do. They talked about it every day and made no moves other than standing still.

"As soon as I get relieved, Davis took almost everybody up to the cemetery to inspect it. So once they get back we'll be breaking up into shifts."

Susan and Dane walked over to the rest of the guys who looked tired as hell. The scent of coffee gave their eyes a tiny bright spot, as if a cup of coffee somehow meant that all was not lost. They opened the thermoses and sipped slowly: this was the highlight of the last few hours and they were not about to gulp it down and be left with nothing.

As if they needed to be reminded that all was not well, a stench rode in on the wind. It smelled like sulfur, or sewer steam, it was faint, but in the air all the same. The scent didn't go away either: it hung over them, it clung to them. They wondered where the stench came from.

The thought was answered as Dane, without realizing, began spilling his coffee onto his shoes. His mouth was agape, as was Susan's. The chubby cop, Sal, jumped up and grabbed his rifle. His eyes peered through the scope seeing what the rest could only guess was slowly coming up the street. It was a grey, decaying, mob of things that used to people. It was the walking dead: the kind of dead that shouldn't exist but did regardless, the kind that stood upright, craving living flesh. And there they were, making their way to New Haven.

Dane grabbed his talkie, "We've got more coming! Requesting immediate backup!" His voice was thick with panic.

"Sal, how many are there?" Asked Jones, shotgun in hand.

"Don't know, must be a hundred easy," he handed Jones the rifle. "Take a look for your self and let me know I'm not loosing my mind."

Jones reassured him. There were at least a hundred dead things shambling toward town. They stayed close together for the most part, with only a few smaller clusters off to either side, and a few trailing behind. Jones could see that one of the creatures was dragging its intestines on the ground, foot upon foot of ropey innards, with not so much as a scowl. He nearly vomited. The sheer number of them was surreal. They had encountered the dead things a number of times, but never like this. This was an army of the dead.

"Shoot at will! We'll be there when we can!" Sheriff Davis snapped, "Over."

"Make it quick! Over and out," Dane replied.

Sal started picking them off one by one. They were too far away for him to be accurate with their shots. The wind, coupled with the distance the bullet would have to travel made it tough for even a trained sniper to accurately hit his mark. Dane rushed Susan to her car. He told her to get home, lock all the doors and windows. Then he promised he'd be there just as soon as he could. She reluctantly got into her car but drove off in a hurry.

24

Dane and the rest of the men grabbed their guns. Dane hopped into his cruiser and took off down the road to get closer and no one objected. Sal thought it was a good idea and did the same. They got close enough to make their shots count, and began picking them off at a decent clip. But they still kept coming. They knew they had fewer bullets than targets and if backup didn't show up before they ran out, they'd be fucked.

They held their position and kept firing. Dane wasn't nearly as good a shot with a rifle as Sal, so he opted to grab his shotgun and drive in even closer. Sal was stunned to see Dane do such a thing: he'd never been the type to pull cowboy stunts, and Dane was far more cautious than that. He watched in awe as Dane got dangerously close to the dead things, close enough to blast three of them in the face with his shotgun.

As he headed off-road to loop around he nailed one with the front end of his cruiser. The foul-smelling creature was struck at an angle that dragged it below the underbelly of the car, popping its head like a bottle under the wheel. He did this a few more times, eventually thinning the heard by seven. After Dane was finished with his unusual antics he headed back to the roadblock and positioned his car where it had been previously. Jones never left his spot and had only fired a few shots. He was on the walkie-talkie with Davis. They were only minutes away.

The creatures weren't discouraged in the slightest and continued to creep forward. It looked like they'd be past the roadblock any minute. Sal was still up ahead and shooting, but quickly got in his cruiser, as a few of the creatures began hurrying toward him. Their dead muscles tearing with every step, they got to the car just as Sal closed the door. He sped off and managed to knock them to the ground with the tail of his cruiser.

Jones squeezed off shot after shot with his shaky hands and somehow, by the grace of God he thought, hit his marks. But, with every walking corpse they put down, another came into view. The officers stood their ground in front of the roadblock, making as many shots count as possible. But the creatures continued to close the distance. The stench of their rotting bodies could make a garbage truck scream, or maggot-ridden chunks of beef smell like perfume on a stripper's tits. They were close enough now to see the flesh being punctured by the spray of bullets. The muzzle flashes highlighted their grayish blue skin, illuminating the bullet-ridden flesh.

Dane wondered what had brought them to New Haven. Was it the fall foliage or the spacious fields? Had they devoured the rest of the county and come looking for more? Tires screeched behind the roadblock, shaking Dane from his thoughts.

Davis and his men drove up in a fury with guns blazing. He was driving his own pickup and the back was full of locals and their peacemakers. The creatures spread out, clustering towards the closest prey. The dead things seemed to be moving quicker now that a meal ticket was in reach. Davis was doing donuts around them, taking a few out with his fender every time.

One got wrapped up in the wheel well causing the truck to jerk unexpectedly. Jones watched the tail end of the truck in horror as one of the guys went flying out of the back. Two of the other guys tried to grab him but their attempt almost sent them out as well. Before he even hit the ground, vicious undead marauders were on him, pulling at him.

The poor son of a bitch was Roger, one of Davis's fishing buddies!

Roger fired at blurry hands as he fell but was bitten at the waist. He screamed. The gang in the back of the truck fired as best they could. Then one of the men shot Roger in the head. Whether it was on purpose, or an accident, it put Roger out of his misery. He wouldn't be able to feel the teeth and fingers digging out his guts and plucking out his eyes to feast upon. Once his warm flesh began to cool, however, the dead things let his corpse lie, unable to sleep. Moments later, Roger, a pile of unrecognizable shredded flesh, complete with a hole in his head, got up and joined the ranks of the dead.

Dane's expression grew grim. His only desire was to get home to Susan, pop on the television and watch nothing remotely interesting as the aroma of fresh coffee filtered in from the kitchen. Those daydreams came to a quick end when the gristle and gray matter started spattering on his cruiser. A scream came from the right of where Dane was standing. It was punctuated by the sounds of gunfire and the grunting of the dead, but it was a scream nonetheless. Dane couldn't see who it was. His vision was blurred and he was close to passing out. So much madness in such a short time, it was hell and hell was getting really hot.

Most of the men never had to fire their weapons at anything other than targets and bottles, yet they were now putting holes into heads. Some found they enjoyed it, the violence was so addictive and enthralling. For most, though, death stayed a taboo, one big question mark at the end of a life. Killing was now a right of passage for the men of the new world if they planned to survive.

More screams broke the monotony of the gunfire. Someone else had fallen, another guy Davis had coerced into bearing arms against the living dead. There were few dead things left and with a few well-placed shots the numbers finally dwindled to zero.

Alan began torching the remains of the creatures and the few who fell victim to them. Thick black smoke rose from the ground. The smell was awful. Dane wiped his sweaty forehead, pulling chunks of flesh, and dried blood off him. He wanted to go home and shower, wrap his arms around Susan and feel like a human being again. Instead he felt like a hollowed out husk, a rusty robot in dire need of oil and lubrication.

Davis grabbed his talkie, his leathered face covered in sweat. "South Roadblock come in." He paused, waiting for a reply.

"Sheriff, this is south. What's up?"

"How you guys holding up? We just had ourselves a helluva firefight."

"What? Is everyone okay?" the voice from the other end asked.

"No, we lost a few guys...we're going to need something more than a roadblock if more of these fuckers come to town. Get your guys and meet me at George's lot," said Davis.

"See ya there. Over."

All the men at the North roadblock were either huddled together or else in their vehicles as Davis pulled up. He opened his door, standing a head above his truck while using the door for leverage, "Listen up," he yelled, "Finish torching these dead fucks and everyone, and I mean EVERYONE, meet me at George's lot! This shit's only begun."

***

Jeff had just finished his sandwich, dipping his last bit of roll into some hummus. His father had a room temperature bottle of Budweiser lingering off his lip. The kids were eating peanut butter and jelly. Apart from everyone chewing, the only sound you could hear was the wind crashing against the boarded-up windows. Barbara and Maria were eating some pasta left over from the night before and Laura was having a bit of everything. Barbara was tense and wanted to say something, she actually wanted to breakdown and cry, but she kept herself in check. The adults had agreed to keep cool in front of the kids (there was no need to scare them more than they already were). And they'd be in bed soon enough, leaving the adults to talk and curse and cry all they wanted. Lunch was a late one and should have been called dinner.

Walter and Jeff went out to the porch, beers in hand, and looked up at the sky. It was almost dark.

Walter looked at his son. "Let's take a stroll around the house. Give it one last look." He put the beer up to his lip and kicked it back.

Jeff followed suit and they both took a casual walk around the house. All the boards looked good, and there was nothing in the distance besides the faint scent of smoke. A drop of rain fell, then another. A line of cars passed the road in the distance, Davis's pickup leading the way. A rumble was heard in the sky, lightning struck and thunder rolled.

Jeff and his father finished up their walk around and ended right back on the porch. Walter looked up at the sky and Jeff looked at his father. Jeff's son, Tommy, came out to the porch as well. Jeff put his arm around him and pulled him closer. He had no idea what was going on, but he sure loved a thunderstorm.

Everyone one was back in the family room with their stomachs full. The rain started to come down heavier, it wasn't pouring, but it was more than a trickle on the roof. The kids were getting antsy, so Maria decided to bring them upstairs. She took a big flashlight and led the way. She lit a few candles on the way to the room as well, and another inside the room so the kids wouldn't get too scared. Just for peace-of-mind she left the flashlight with them. Tommy grabbed it and gave it to Sandra, and then Sandra gave it to little Wally.

They weren't quite ready for bed so they started building a fort and playing with their toys. Maria sat in the room and just watched. She loved them so much, and couldn't bear to think about what may lay ahead for them.

They started building a fort around her as Sandra sat on her lap making goofy faces with the flashlight under her chin. Maria started laughing and crying at the same time. Maria wrapped her arms around Sandra and tackled the rest of them into the halfway-built fort and brought the sheets down with her. You could hear the laughter from the family room. The others smiled. The rain continued to fall.

4 THE ROAD TO HELL

The two groups sat together in the warehouse on pallets and crates, exchanging ideas and information. Ben's group was small; there were only two others, a guy that worked at Mal-Mart, Chung-Hee, and a fellow truck driver, Shorty, whom he picked up along the way. Shorty was an older man with a big goatee and tattoos over most of his visible skin, Chung-Hee was in his late teens, Korean, and he wore glasses and looked fairly athletic. Ben and Shorty, who clearly was not short, had been on the road since day one. Shorty was on his short band radio calling for help after his truck ran out of gas when Ben got the call and made the trip to get him. By the time Ben got there Shorty was on top of the truck with his bag, wearing his unloading gloves and swinging a crowbar at every dead hand that reached for him. Ben pulled up alongside the truck, mowing down some of the creatures in the process. Shorty nearly fell as he jumped onto the hood of the cab and Ben told him to hold on as they went down the road a bit, before could get inside the truck safely.

The next day they docked at the seemingly vacant store and came across Chung-Hee, who had been surviving up on the roof and in some isolated parts of the store. After getting together, the trio had been working together to gather up whatever supplies they could.

"I'm telling' you, the safe zones are bullshit deathtraps," Ben yelled.

"It's the best thing to do, there's a group of us, and with a lot of kids--" Gerty defended, before getting cut off.

"To get to the closest military guarded safe zone from here would mean going into Titan City, or Haddonfield. Both of which would be suicide," Ben said.

"Let's not forget, that any bridge at this point would be totally fucked, not to mention the tunnel," Shorty added.

"No matter where we go we'll have to use a bridge eventually," Eddie chimed in.

"Either way you cut it, it's a raw deal. But the way I see it, I can only count on ME to look out for me" Ben said, his eyes pleading. "Do you really think the government can take care of us? We gotta take care of ourselves."

"Look, we're at the campgrounds," Gerty said. "You're more than welcome to come and join us before you split, and we can all talk some more. We should get out of here." Then as she turned and headed back and the further she moved away from him the better she felt.

"Hey, wait a minute! Are there any weapons in the store?" Frankie asked.

"Yeah. Not much. By layaway… but be careful: there are more of those deaders around," Chung-Hee said.

"I'll go with you, I can't believe I didn't think of that earlier," Shorty said, feeling stupid.

"I'm going to keep loading the truck," Ben said. "I think we'll follow you guys to your camp, so swing around when you're ready, if you don't mind. Hopefully I can talk you out of a death sentence."

"Not a problem," Eddie replied.

Shorty and Frankie had made it to the sporting goods section near the layaway department, Jon-Jon and Dawn following along. The glass showcases were smashed. Jon-Jon walked around looking at the area; he saw no signs of lurkers, or deaders as Chung-Hee called them. Frankie rummaged through the cases and only found three small knives. Behind the counter was a row of locked storage compartments. Shorty broke the locks with his crowbar, revealing a treasure trove of hunting knives. Jon-Jon came across some hunting and archery gear. He picked up a Crossbow and whatever arrows he could find. He also grabbed a few Compound Bows and whatever other bows were lying around. He wasn't sure what went with what, but figured someone at the campgrounds would know what to do with them. Dawn was looking through the hunting gear. She put on a camouflage cap and continued looking. Gerty came from around the corner of an aisle with Eddie, Frankie, and Joseph. They had bags upon bags around their shoulders.

Eddie looked at Jon-Jon's haul and smiled, "crossbow?"

"Hell, yeah."

"Nice."

Eddie headed toward the layaway area, which was just beyond the showcases. He slowly crept up to the dim area, passing a return rack. He peeked into the area, locating the doors: two were clearly bathrooms, and the other for an employee lounge. He sniffed the air and whatever crawled up his nose told him to quickly back up and leave. He did just that, if he learned anything lately, it was to trust his instincts.

"We need to get out of here," Eddie said, almost whispering, but was clearly serious.

"What's up?" Asked his brother, Joseph.

"I can smell them, who knows how many are back there? Let's just fuckin' go! We got plenty of shit," Eddie insisted.

They followed behind him, no arguments, jogging as quietly as possible. Eddie popped through the doors, startling Ben who was quick to pull his gun, which in turn stopped Eddie in his tracks. Chung-Hee looked whiter than a ghost, but ready to bolt if need be.

"Sorry didn't mean to scare you guys, just wanted to let you know we're getting the hell outta here," Eddie said. "We'll meet you out back in a few."

"All right, thanks. We'll be waiting," Ben said, as he put his gun down.

Shorty came through the door with a gun tucked into his pants, his crowbar in hand and a hunter's bag slung over his shoulder. Ben and Chung-Hee were done and pulling the door down. Eddie took off out the door and headed toward the entrance where Big Cups was waiting the whole time. The gang followed behind, Gerty at the rear. When they reached the door Big Cups was standing against the wall, his breath smelled of peanut butter and chocolate but his expression was not of satisfaction but of total fear. He dropped the walkie-talkie and everybody could clearly see why. In the distance was a sea of grey—a virtual army of the dead, ranks upon ranks of them. Groans and grunts filled the air. Joseph grabbed the walkie-talkie and headed toward the vehicles, as did the rest of them.

As they reached the rear of store where they were to meet Ben, Shorty, and Chung-Hee, they heard the moans grow louder and now could smell the lurking bastards. Ben heard it too, and Chung-Hee grew whiter still, though any whiter he'd be a sheet of paper. Shorty just looked tired, the hard lines of his face sat like gouges.

"Lead the way!" Shorty yelled to them.

Frankie was halfway out of the parking lot. Gerty followed behind in the new SUV, and Ben was right on her ass. Ben looked in the oversized rear view mirror that barely hung to the driver's side of the truck. His jaw hit the floor and came back up in time to help his lower lip quiver. He was seeing the sea of grey behind him washing over the parking lot where they had just been. The dead were in the street as well, probably in the woods too, but it was too hard to tell. They were everywhere.

"Boone, you there?" Asked Joseph, in the SUV with Gerty.

"Yeah, how you guys making out?"

"Not good, we got like a million lurkers behind us. Any sign of them there?" he asked.

"It's been clear, why?"

"Make sure you guys are ready to leave—they just came out of nowhere, they're everywhere!" Joseph replied "They're a few miles behind us now, but I don't think we should stick around."

"Fuck. All right, shit. How far away are you?"

"Maybe…ten minutes, maybe a little less. We're moving pretty fast," Joseph said.

"Tell that idiot not to get everybody worked up!" Gerty shouted.

"Yeah, yeah, shhh," Joseph gestured to her with his hand to shut up.

"What was that?" Boone asked.

"Nothing, just keep everyone calm, over." Joseph put the walkie-talkie down.

"Easier said than done, over and out."

The three vehicles raced toward the camp. For most, the thought of reaching the Titan City safe zone seemed like an unrealistic possibility. At first, they thought it would be no problem, but now, just surviving was proving to be harder and harder. The creatures now crept from the road and direction they planned to take to get there. It was a possibility that these creatures all came from Titan City. However, there are plenty of other cities, and towns they could be from. By the looks of them it may have been the whole county. Few options remained for the group, but they were insistent on continuing with their initial plan, despite how difficult it would be, especially now.

The creatures appeared to be staggering from the direction they needed to go. That alone raised a number of red flags and many questions that would remain unanswered. Most of the group couldn't stay where they were. Many had to flee, some were found, and others hope to find loved ones at Titan City, and other places along the way. Many towns organized their own safe zones at churches, schools, even hotels. But news reports stated that they were becoming overcrowded, and even had violent situations develop as a result.

The media outlets would eventually report that the safest course of action was to stay home. Gerty had to flee her home, and sought sanctuary at her church. When she pulled up to it, people were banging on the door to get in. She drove off as soon as she heard the gunshots.

Some of the other travelers had similar stories. Others left their homes to shack up with nearby relatives only to find them dead and hungry on arrival. Others had no real reason for traveling with the group other than to be a part of something, they were caught in the moment but the moment hadn't ended.

Everyone had stories.

It had been days, closing in on weeks since anyone had seen a live television broadcast and days since a live radio broadcast. They had been sporadic since the start, the last one ending abruptly just over a day ago. The last of the media coverage coupled with everyone's experiences over the last few days would lead one, or all, to suggest that going ahead to a safe zone was not the safest idea, nor was it the best solution. With the media coverage suggesting staying home as the best thing to do, and everyone knew people who did so, but most of them just couldn't see going back home as a solution either. Some had to run from their homes. For many it was too late to turn back, and the heart doesn't know what the head does. They might be headed down the wrong path but with enough perseverance and hope they can turn the wrong path into the right one. Or, the devil be damned, survive it.

Boone, for the most part, was the group's leader–a role he fell into. It wasn't something he felt comfortable with at first, if at all, but it wasn't his choice anymore. He spoke his mind and everything he said just made perfect sense. So when he told the people at the camp to be ready to move out in ten minutes, they listened. Boone stood, holding a shotgun, in front of the hodgepodge of a convoy that was lined up and ready to roll out. Next to Boone were Sarah and Milah, his immediate traveling companions. Scott and Judy walked up to the three of them. They seemed almost unaffected by their situation, maybe it was acceptance of it, but it was something that most people found off putting. Boone thought that they were probably this way before the dead forgot how to die, and he found it reassuring, as if he could've known them then. Scott and Judy came to Boone with a small idea, and he thought it was a good one.

The three vehicles raced up the path toward Boone and the others. Frankie parked and jumped out of his truck. Gerty did the same. Eventually almost everyone was out of their vehicles again and crowding around.

"What's going on, guys?" Judy asked.

"There's gotta be a thousand of those things, maybe more," Frankie said wildly.

"Thousands," Boone barely whispered.

"We've got plenty of time to get out of here, but the thing is…they're coming from the direction we want to go," Gerty said, "Which means plan A is fucked, and I don't recall hearing a plan B."

Everyone nodded in agreement. Scott followed up with, "well, we don't really have any choice, do we? We have to go back…or run right through them, either way…"

"We're not running right through them! That would be suicide," Frankie said, cutting him off.

"So we have to go back the other way, but before we go…I think we should set fire to the brush," Scott said. "They'll walk right into it and it could buy us some extra time."

"How do you plan on doing that," Gerty said sarcastically.

"We do have a pretty big bonfire over there," Judy said as she pointed toward the pile of burning cadavers and tree branches.

"We need to worry about getting everybody out of here first," Frankie, becoming irritated, said as he looked at the rest of the group standing by their vehicles.

"What's going on," yelled a woman's voice, as she stepped out of her car.

"It's okay, Jan, we're just figuring out where to go," Frankie said.

She didn't look very satisfied and Frankie knew if they didn't figure something out, this would become a very sticky situation. "Look, we need to get out of here now, we passed a liquor store before we set up camp here, maybe a half hour down the road. Let's go there and figure out something better."

"Ah, shit, did you hear that?" Gerty said, looking around. "Get in your cars, and follow Frank. Let's go!"

"Boone, I'm sticking with my idea: Judy and me are gonna light this place up," Scott said as he ran towards the fire.

"Hurry the fuck up, and watch yer ass," Boone said, running to his car.

Jon-Jon ran to his van as Dawn followed behind. Scott grabbed a tree branch full of flaming leaves and tossed it into the thick of the woods, igniting the fallen leaves on the ground. Judy did the same. The leaves began to burn and the crackling of fire began to fill the night air. Frankie was heading back down the path with a convoy behind him. Scott and Judy now had a significant blaze going, nothing that compared to their current bonfire, but it was something.

The last of the vehicles pulled out and down the path. Scott and Judy continued to spread the fire along the brush. Some patches took while others died out or else blew away. Judy ran to their little car, an early hybrid. It used to be a bright blue, but that was no longer the case. She started it up and drove it toward the path. She got out and left the door slightly open. Judy was getting very nervous.

The fire was climbing the trees as the sickly smell of rotted meat crawled up her nose. She knew the smell all too well, even before the dead came back to life she'd come to know that smell. It was rot. She recalled one of the few cadavers she ever worked on. It was summer. The man had gotten so drunk that he fell off his balcony and broke his neck on the way down. He landed behind a row of bushes and laid there for three days before anyone noticed. His neighbors didn't notice he was missing, just that there was a terrible smell. His neighbor thought the smell came from a dead animal. When she found out it was the man from upstairs she was aghast. She never knew the man, but if you asked her if she did, she'd probably tell you 'no' but that she knew he liked to have fun (and maybe he had a bit too much fun the night he fell).

"I think we should go," she said, and went back to the car, throwing another burning branch into the woods.

"Right behind you, babe," Scott had a flaming branch in each hand. He ran them down a bit farther and tossed them. He turned and ran to the car. He hopped into the passenger side and Judy pressed the pedal to the floor.

She raced down the path, sweating, Scott too, he wiped his brow. Judy started screaming. At first Scott looked at her, then looked ahead at the path. There were lurkers coming out of the woods. Many of them were seminude, their clothes and skin were shredded, both hanging on in desperate clumps and clots.

"Gun it, don't stop!" Scott yelled.

She listened, plowing two of them over, one of them leaving some of its rotting face on the windshield; skin off of its cheekbone and the dried up gelatin of its yellowed eyes. Judy kept up her speed, although the handling on the woodland ground was far from ideal. But she managed to keep the car on the path. She hit another, and another, as the blood and gristle covered the windshield. She flicked on the wipers and they did a wonderful job of smearing it around without wiping it off. She couldn't see any of the damage that the dead things had done to her car, but she could feel it in the handling.

Nearing the end of the path, she fishtailed onto the road and could see thirty or forty of them lumbering forward, which was just the tip of the iceberg. Dead fingers scraped at the windows as Judy sped away.

"Whoo!" Scott yelled, his grin going from ear to ear.

"Oh, my God, oh, my God, oh, my God," is all Judy could say.

"That was fuckin' crazy!" he said as he put his hand over his chest to feel the rapid beating of his heart.

Her foot was pressed to the floor, and their little car sped along. The windshield wipers were finally starting to clear some of the gunk off. The dim yellow streetlights made the blood smears look like yellow mud. There were chunks of gristle on the grill, around the headlights, the rearview mirrors and even the sides of the car were caked in blood.

They pulled up to the liquor store. Everyone else from the group was outside of their cars and in the midst of a harried group discussion. The kids were sitting in the back of Frankie's pick up and inside Jon-Jon's van, just out of earshot. Everyone turned to look when Scott and Judy pulled in, they continued looking when they saw how bloody the vehicle had become.

"What the hell happened?" Boone asked.

"They were right on top of us, as soon as we started down the trail, they were everywhere," Judy said.

"We were maybe two minutes behind the rest of you guys and then bam, out of nowhere," Scott finished for her.

"Shit, they're moving quicker than we thought," said Ben.

"Who the hell are you?" Scott asked the new guy.

"Ben. We were at the store, met up with your friends there," Ben told him. He held his palm up to point out Shorty and Chung-Hee.

"Oh, okay, sorry, didn't mean to sound like a dick," Scott mumbled.

"Okay, so they're still on our ass," Eddie said.

"…and we're still no better off than before," Frankie headed towards his truck.

"What about those office buildings down the way?" Judy asked.

"Nah, we'd really have to check it out before jumping inside," Boone said.

"He's right, we have to go further. We'd need time to check a place out…could walk into a deathtrap," Eddie insisted.

"Can we fight 'em? Are there really that many…we got guns," Ricker chimed in.

"Ricker, that would be crazy," Boone snapped.

"It's not that crazy…maybe…" Jon-Jon muttered.

"Get the fuck outta here, you seen how many there were," Gerty clenched her meaty fists.

"I'm serious. There's that truck stop not too far from here, just past the office buildings, we can rig that big propane tank to blow and that could set off the pumps," Jon-Jon continued.

"That's fucking crazy and stupid!" Gerty's knuckles turned white as she squeezed her fists tighter.

"I never said it wasn't, but so is being chased by fucking zombies," Jon-Jon replied.

"Please don't call them that, it creeps me out. Zombies can't be real. Those people must have a disease or something," Judy said.

"Save the debate for later. Jon, maybe you're right…it's not that bad of an idea," Boone said, "its crazy enough, it just might work."

"What?" Gerty was dumbfounded.

"If we can kill enough of them… maybe we can pass them. If not, we can still try for the city. There are many small towns up ahead, too that we can drive through and maybe get around those things. We already know what's behind us," Boone continued.

"Ain't nothing behind us," Ricker added, spitting on the ground, "nothing but dead ends," he added with a morbid smile.

"What do we have to lose?" Boone asked.

Despite the lack of any unanimous decision, the group headed for the truck stop. There was certainly the chance that the truck stop would be out of fuel and low on propane. But without much of an alternative Jon-Jon and Boone persuaded the others to see it through. How they managed to do so, neither could figure out. It seemed with each passing day people were willing to do things they wouldn't have a day prior.

While passing the section of office buildings in enroute to the truck stop Gerty slowed down to take a look. She noticed a few cars still in the lot and a door to one of the buildings was wide open. A bloody handprint led from the middle of the door to the ground and caught between the door and its frame was a body; a swollen, twisted, mangled mess of a body. There were a few other buildings that looked vacant but would need a much closer inspection before consideration. And time was an unfriendly neighbor with nowhere to be but at your throat.

Jon-Jon slowed to a crawl, peering out the window and surveying the truck stop. There were several cars he hadn't noticed when they initially passed it. Upon closer inspection, inside the attached eatery, staring back, were another group of survivors. Stealing the spotlight for a moment was yet another group of people, separate from the group of people in the eatery, coming from out of the small store, the Quick Stop, located toward the rear of the pumps. This new group consisted of three men, all of which were running toward a car parked just outside the store's door. They were carrying out what looked like beef jerky, chips, handfuls of other fine eatery, a few maps, and cartons of cigarettes. It all dropped to the ground as they noticed Jon-Jon's van and the band of vehicles behind him approaching. Two out of the three guys pulled out handguns from their waists. The third jumped into the car with his findings wrapped tightly in his hands. Jon-Jon opened the door to his van very slowly and stepped out cautiously. He raised his hands, standing next to his van. Boone did the same, only he had his gun drawn, Frankie did the same. Ben and Shorty pulled out their guns and joined the party. Ben's eyes turned to narrow slits as he examined the three men.

"We're not looking for trouble fellas," Jon-Jon spoke loud and clear to the three men facing him.

"Neither are we," said the guy who jumped into the car.

"Why don't we all lower our guns then, and have a chat," said Jon-Jon. "Where you guys headed to?"

"Headed to Briggstown, you?" The guy in the car said.

"We were headed toward Titan City, but there's a shit-load of dead fuckers down the road between us and the road we need to be on," Jon-Jon explained.

"You could just drive right through them things," said the tall guy who drew his gun first.

"When I say a shit-load, I mean a fucking shit-load, maybe even a few thousand," Jon-Jon put it poetically.

"No shit?" The tall man asked.

"No shit, man, we were thinking we might be able to use this station to blast them to hell and continue on our merry fucking way," Jon-Jon continued. "This is the only road we can travel down, everything else if fucked unless we wanted to travel by foot."

"Yeah, man…it's a fucking mess out there, but if you want to blast a hole in them things, we're down. We sure as hell ain't going back the other way, we lost…we lost everyone two days ago, man," the tall man confided.

"Then we better get a move on, before they catch up," Boone finally contributed.

Boone directed everyone to drive past the truck stop, far enough for a big blast. Jon-Jon kept his van at the station so he and the others that were going to ignite the tanks could get away safely. They approached the folks at the eatery and they were more than happy to accompany the plan. They were just happy to see other people and be a part of something bigger than hiding at a truck stop—there was hope in numbers, even if hope died fast. They drove up to join the others, passed what they thought would be a safe distance. Eddie and Joseph hung outside the vehicles and kept an eye out for lurkers while they introduced themselves to the newcomers.

Boone, Jon-Jon, Ben, Shorty, Damian, Corey, who was the tall man, and Julio, the man who jumped into the car, stayed at the truck stop to figure out how they could blow it up. They came to the realization that either way they did it, it would be a messy, dangerous miracle. Not a single person in the group knew what to do. Their collective experience with explosives ended at fireworks and began at the movies. Excessive heat would blow the propane tank, that much was stated on the side of the tank by means of a set of warning stickers. They figured if they doused the stop with enough gasoline the place would ignite and eventually explode. Ben mentioned shooting at the propane tank from a distance and they all agreed that seemed to be the best approach.

"I can see them! They're coming!" Gerty screamed.

Jon-Jon and Boone looked at each other, exchanging an entire conversation with a gaze. They ran to the pumps and tried to pry the hoses free from their dispensing units. The effort was fruitless. Boone pulled out a small, but razor-sharp, fillet knife from his pocket and began cutting the hose. The hose cut easily enough and Boone continued to work through the rest of them. Jon-Jon and the rest of the guys ran over to the convoy where anyone with a gun was standing in the street facing the approaching flesh eaters. The gasoline flowed into the street creating a small river between the living and the living dead.

To Boone's surprise the hoses refused to release any more of their precious liquid and he ran over to the rest of them with his eyebrows arched in full disbelief. Ben met him halfway and explained.

"The dispenser units only hold so much gas, the rest has to be pumped from the tanks underground," Ben said.

"Shit," Boone replied.

"We're gonna have to hope blowing the propane tank does the trick and blows the main tanks below sky high," Ben yelled.

"Guess so," Boone said, then turned to the rest of the gang and yelled "everyone get back in your cars and start moving back. We're gonna blow the tank."

They listened. Ben, Damian, Boone, and Jon-Jon stayed behind. They used Jon-Jon's van to shield themselves from whatever would happen once they began shooting at the tank. They waited till the dead things staggered closer. Every second felt like a season and after ten minutes the dead things were upon the station. They took aim, counted to three, and then fired. They didn't have time to shield their faces as a small 'tink' sound turned into a furious blast leveling most of the truck stop and sending the four men onto the street with their legs in the air and the wind knocked out of their lungs. As they stumbled to their feet, the rest of the truck stop crumpled to the ground. The fire took to the gasoline and the streets began to burn as the flesh-eating creatures staggered closer.

Jon-Jon struggled to get to his van, a piece of shrapnel from the tank had grazed his leg, making it painful to walk. He pulled himself into the drivers seat as the rest of them wearily climbed inside the van.

The unscathed creatures were now mere feet from the van, the ones that walked into the fire melted with each step forward. Their eyes and lips burned off right away as did their clothing. They resembled charred mummies now instead of people. Jon-Jon whipped his van around and sped away toward the convoy. The convoy had slowed to a crawl and eventually stopped by the time Jon-Jon had caught up to it. Boone hopped out of the vehicle to see what the hold up was and as he did, he found out that he didn't need to ask. One of the cars from the eatery addition had crashed into Gerty's SUV and pinned her and the rest of her passengers between Scott and Judy's little trash can on wheels. The driver of the car was feasting on his passenger as two people in the backseat were trying to get out. Gerty and her passengers were trapped, as was Judy, and Scott lie slumped on the steering wheel with blood coming from his nose.

Boone stepped closer to the scene with his gun drawn. Ben and Damian stepped out of the van and covered the rear, making sure nothing crept up on them. Jon-Jon kept his ass in his seat, moving his eyes from rear view mirror to the view just outside the windshield. Boone was now to the side of the car that started the commotion. The two in the backseat had managed to get out of the car and Boone directed them to the van but they opted for the closest seat of an obliging driver. He took another step forward, his gun leading the way and put two shots in the passenger's head. Most of her throat was ripped out and dangling from the mouth of the man behind the wheel. He made eye contact with Boone and Boone held its gaze for a moment, wondering if anything human was behind its cold stare. Deciding that it didn't matter, he put two in his head as well. He walked over to Scott, who was now waking up with Judy screaming into his ear. He recognized Boone, despite how blurry he appeared, and gave him a thumb up. Scott moved his car to the side, allowing Gerty enough room to get the convoy rolling again. Damian had begun to squeeze off a few rounds as the things staggered closer and closer. The creatures had never looked more alike then now. Though the fire in the street had died down, they were the color of smoke, much of their bodies were burned and one could easily confuse them with skeletons. Ben took a few shots too. Headshots every time, he did it calmly and made it look easy. It was clear he knew his way around a weapon. A huge second blast rocked forth from the truck stop as the tanks below the surface finally ignited. The blast was blinding and scorched a large number of the dead creatures. The blast leveled many of the dead troopers and sent others flying into the air; their lifeless limbs flaking off their charred bodies. Once the smoke cleared, more soldiers of the dead army stepped forward to replenish their ranks.

The flames in the rear view continued to burn bright and hot as Boone directed the convoy past the mess in the road. He contemplated getting into the bloodied vehicle and moving it but thought better of it when he saw not an inch of seat that wasn't covered in blood. The cars slowly maneuvered around the wreckage and made their way up the road. Dozens upon dozens of the stiff legged creatures hobbled onto the road from out of the woods. Big Cups had his arm hanging out the window when one of the creatures wrapped its crooked-toothed maw around it and bit down. Big Cups thrashed in his seat and screamed as the creature pulled a mouthful of flesh from his small arm. Another two creatures crept up to the window wanting a taste as well. His screams alerted everyone in earshot but they couldn't do much more than drive away. The road was soon full of the bloodthirsty creatures. Cups was dragged from the window as his car sped away, and Ricker, in the back seat with him, was too scared to do anything but whimper. He simply watched as Cups kicked and screamed and then finally disappeared.

Another car from the group at the eatery swerved into a ditch on the side of the road, trying to avoid several other lurkers that appeared from the side of the road. The dead things were clawing at their windows. The driver aimed her gun at one of them and fired a shot into its head, hitting her mark. Unfortunately, though, the bullet broke the window and the other dead things got inside before she could make another shot count.

The others attempted to flee but couldn't move past the dead weight of their attackers. They screamed for help and for God but neither showed up. They died slowly as dead mouths tore the skin from their bodies. Boone ran to Jon-Jon's van and jumped in as Frankie's truck swerved off the road and spun out of control. They sped up to them as Boone and Damian jumped out of the vehicle with guns drawn. Ben poked half his body out the window and fired his weapon several times, only half his shots hitting anything of worth. Frankie, Eddie and Joseph climbed out of the truck as Damian kicked one of the creatures back and down. He put his foot on the creature's throat and fired three shots into the dead things head. Boone shot one that was creeping up behind them and Frankie fired his shotgun and took down three more that were approaching the truck.

Frankie ran around the front of the vehicle to see why he lost control of his truck and when he did he almost lost control of his stomach. He fought to hold back the vomit that was climbing his esophagus as he aimed his gun at a creature that was wrapped up and mangled in his truck's wheel-well. A mangled arm reached for Frankie and he shot it, though he couldn't imagine how the thing would ever get itself unwound and mobile. The axle was wrecked and Frankie punched his truck, twisting his wrist in the process. The three of them gathered what they could and ran toward the van as Ben popped out of the window again to give them some covering fire.

With the van full, Jon-Jon pressed down hard on the pedal and sped up to the rest of the convoy. Ben kept himself half out of the van and tried to shoot a few more of the lurking creatures but each shot failed to reach its intended target. His shots were as wild as his eyes. He hung out of the window like a dog, even his tongue hung out slightly.

The convoy drove for nearly an hour, passing what had become the usual wreckage of abandoned cars and ransacked strip malls.

Occasionally a lone lurking flesh eater would stagger into view and quickly vanish in a trail of dust and exhaust fumes. Eventually the road forked and they would have to decide on taking route 287 or taking route 519 into Union County and hope for the best. Shorty and Chung-Hee had been in the lead and pulled to the side of the road leaning toward 519, they waited there till the rest of the convoy was gathered. After very little discussion route 519 was chosen and Jon-Jon led the procession into Union County.

5 GOOD INTENTIONS

It was getting darker out now, and the heavy foliage made it even darker. Jon-Jon eased the van down the road and took the exit for Mill Creek and continued to head west on Dry River Road. They drove past a 'Welcome to Mill Creek' sign that was in desperate need of repair or replacement.

Under light of the moon buildings became visible. The first of which was some sort of print shop that looked more like a warehouse. The parking lot was empty and there was a wire fence separating it from the woods behind it. They drove past it and soon found themselves in the middle of what looked like the main street. But it wasn't called Main Street, it was called Broadway and it was littered with newspapers, and glass from the broken windows of the storefronts.

Beyond the ruined storefront windows were the ransacked innards of what could've been fancy shops and quaint corner delis at one point. Calmly parked cars still remained on the street and some shops, which, according to the window signs, were open for business.

There hadn't been any lurkers, or survivors, or even a stray dog, only the emptiness. It was a ghost town plucked from the pages of a western yarn with a modern aesthetic. The convoy passed several cross streets and didn't bother to turn down any of them. Instead, they continued to the end of Broadway, which was marked by the post office. The road then formed a circle around a statue of a firefighter carrying a hose over his shoulder. It looked like copper or tarnished brass, was very large and had benches surrounding its foundation. They too were covered in newspapers and other garbage. The circle opened in the back to reveal a park and the rest of Broadway which appeared every bit the little chunk of suburbia that you'd see portrayed in a television sitcom.

They continued traveling down the road, past the park. Just beyond the park was a school, a modern building with a brick façade. There were two sets of oversized double doors on the front of the building and a fenced in area at the back. Down the road, about a quarter of a mile, was a library, and then the start of a housing development. Anything beyond that was lost in the growing darkness of the evening.

Jon-Jon came to a stop in front of the school and the rest of the convoy followed suit. Jon-Jon, Boone, Eddie and soon a mess of folks gathered on the lawn of the school. Some people were looking for some comforting words or even a pep talk. They didn't get one. Jon-Jon grabbed a flashlight out of his bag and grabbed his pistol. He grabbed Shorty by the shoulder and whispered something in his ear. Jon-Jon then walked away and Shorty followed.

The two of them approached the school. The others talked amongst themselves and paid them no attention. Walking close to each other, they were now at the side of the school building. Jon-Jon shined the light into the first window. It was an office room, perhaps belonging to someone in administration. It looked clear and undisturbed. They moved over to the next window, which was the first in a long series of similar windows. Beyond those windows was a classroom, clean as a whistle, chairs and desks were neatly lined up and even the chalkboard had been washed. With each set of windows it was the same deal. At the back of the building, Jon-Jon leaned into the fence, moving his flashlight back and forth in an attempt to see what—if anything—was beyond the fence. Shorty stood almost on top of him. They could see two soccer goal posts in the distance, and glimmers behind that, which they assumed was the flashlight reflecting off the other end of the fence. All seemed well.

Shorty and Jon-Jon rejoined the group. Jon-Jon turned to his side and noticed a shadow moving to the side of them. He heard the crinkle of leaves and sure enough emerged a dead creature from the darkness. It was a woman, a younger looking woman, who, apart from being dead, didn't appear excessively damaged like many of the other creatures they had encountered. She was almost attractive. She walked with a stagger, and her head twitched violently to one side and back, only to repeat the action again. Without the twitching had one could easily see how the dead things were able to do so much damage: she looked hurt and in need of help, and a few days ago any one of the group would have tried to help her.

Jon-Jon grabbed one of Judy's pipes from her and he turned to face the broken-neck-bitch. He swung into the woman's throat propelling her onto her back. Judy came up from behind Jon-Jon, brandishing her other pipe and began to beat the woman's head into the ground. The two of them mashed her into a puddle of soft mush and red earth. They finished the job before anyone else could be of help. The dead woman's hand continued to twitch as they walked away.

Jon-Jon quickly looked around and noticed a few more moving shadows. He headed for the doors to the school. The others followed. Everyone left their cars carrying whatever they could, crying children included. They needed to put some solid walls between themselves and the creeping shadows of death that seemed to follow them everywhere. If Death himself showed up with a scythe it wouldn't be a surprise. It might even make more sense. The main door was locked, and too solid to try to budge open with a shoulder. They then made a mad dash to the far side of the building that they hadn't checked, but was clear when they drove past it initially. It remained so.

Two dead things started moving toward them from the street. One looked like he could be the custodian of the school. The other was a fat man wearing flannel pajamas and a tank top revealing the gaping wounds in his throat and chest. Dried blood covered the front of his body as well as his exposed arms. Frankie and Eddie took care of the fat man as Damian, Shorty, and Joseph cleaned up the janitor. Jon-Jon continued to the side entrance toward the fence. It was locked as well, but this one had a small rectangular window with chicken wire inside the glass. He looked through the window with his flashlight. It was dark inside, but he didn't see any movement. He started bashing through the window with Judy's pipe. The wire made it difficult, but he broke through it eventually. With Scott and Judy watching his back, Jon-Jon put his hand through the window. He tried to be careful, but even so, he cut and scraped his hand and forearm. By the time he was able to open the door his cuts and scrapes became deep wounds screaming for an infection. He pulled his arm out, nearly crying, and blood flowed profusely from his cuts. Judy gasped and quickly rummaged through her bag, pulling out a spare shirt to wrap around his arm.

The rest of them had finished off the fat man and his friend and caught up just in time to head into the building. Shorty took the lead, as Judy and Scott tightly wrapped Jon-Jon's arm. Boone followed behind Shorty with his flashlight. So far the coast was clear, no noise, no moans, no scratching, only the sounds they themselves made and the silence inside. The door they entered led directly into what the sign next to the door called the A-wing.

Eddie and Frankie were making sure everyone got inside safely and keeping a few eyes out for any of the kids that may have been lost in the shuffle. They'd both seen it happen early on and were not interested in witnessing another occurrence. Once everyone was inside they got together a small group, including the two of them, to scout ahead.

The group consisted of Boone, Shorty, Ben, Eddie, and Frankie. Jon-Jon wanted to go ahead with them but Judy had insisted he not. It was best he take it easy and focus on fully stopping his bloodied arm by resting and applying pressure. They headed down the hall toward the back of the building as the others stood huddled just beyond the door.

Ricker and Dawn were smoking before they could even catch their breath and Jon-Jon took Dawn's side and eventually a few drags of her cigarette. The kids were terrified and lately that was the only expression except exhaustion their faces could seem to muster. Eddie's mother, Janice, was holding together fairly well and took it upon herself to watch over many of the kids. Everybody helped of course—especially Dawn and Gerty—but just helping the kids deal with what was happening was enough to tire anyone out. No one fully understood what was going on. They could only explain what they were seeing but it was hard to explain such things to kids when the ones doing the explaining didn't believe what they were seeing. The best they could hope for was a place of relative safety, and now, they hoped the school would be that place for a little while. Though had any of them been fortune tellers, they would've stayed at home.

They had checked every door going down the corridor and had come up bone-dry in their search for living dead squatters. The corridor wrapped around to the right and on the left was a set of double doors that headed into the cafeteria. They slowly opened the doors and were greeted by a large clean room with a view of the fenced in grounds at the back of the school. Windows went from waist high to a few feet from the ceiling. Tables and chairs were neatly stacked into the corners of the room and on both sides were doors that exited to the grounds. Both doors were locked. Centered between the back exit doors was the kitchen and registers. Beyond the stacks of trays and a series of ordering windows, deep inside the kitchen were three large freezer doors and a giant refrigerator—the only dead things in those were unlabeled meat patties and flattened roaches. They left the large room the same way they entered it and headed to another door that led to the basement.

Boone and his flashlight led the way down the stairs to the lower level. Ben crisscrossed his flashlight's beam over Boone's. Shorty was right behind Ben. Eddie and Frankie held the back of the line. Shorty had his pistol ready in one hand and his crowbar in the other. They stood at the bottom of the steps with their ears listening for noise. Experience had taught them you could sometimes hear a lurker before you'd be able to see one--especially in the dark. Not a sound. They continued into the initial room. Once they began searching the rooms they noted that most of the rooms were for storage; filing cabinets and old desks. They came across a break room that was conveniently labeled 'maintenance only'. The room had some unopened soda bottles and moldy bread on the dirty microwave. The boiler room followed that and it too was labeled as such with a big red sign on the door. They cautiously opened it, Shorty and Ben kept an eye in the other direction. The boiler room was quiet and the pipes weren't hissing or steaming. It was very clean and looked as if the maintenance had, in fact, been maintaining it. Shorty and Ben now stood in the doorway while the others quietly and quickly looked around.

Upstairs, Scott, still dizzy from the collision, along with Judy, Alexis and Joseph, guided the rest of the gang in the opposite direction from Boone and the others, to the gymnasium. Alexis and Joseph had been holding the back of the line. She held a flashlight and had a knife easily accessible in her pocket. Joseph was no more than a foot away and brandished a pistol.

Given the size of the school, the gym was not as big as one would think. Toward the left hand corner of the room was a large stack of gymnastics mats. They were in various sizes and a multitude of colors—all dingy, however. They would make an excellent place to sleep for the night, no one in the group had seen a mattress in some time, and this was the closest they were likely to get any time soon. There was also a rack of basketballs against the wall. To the right of the basketballs was a corridor, which led into the locker rooms. Once they checked and cleared them they headed back into the gym, toward the gym's entrance. After they checked the rest of the floor they came back to the gymnasium.

Scott and Judy waited near the door where they had entered the school, while Alexis and Joseph hung around the gymnasium entrance. They would wait there until the others returned from the basement. There was no other floor and no visible access to the roof.

After a few minutes the group returned from the basement. They met up with Scott and Judy and followed them to the gymnasium.

"Everybody listen up," Boone spoke loudly but not yelling. "We're going to stay the night, it's safe. I think it's best for everyone if we all stay inside."

"Should we just leave our cars the way they are?" Ricker asked.

"Yeah, leave your cars as is for now—so long as they're off, we'll worry about them come daybreak. For now just rest up."

Everyone settled down. There were more than enough mats for everyone to use, and they did. People grouped up and spread out around the gymnasium floor. The children were freaked out being inside the school. They were used to a school being safe, bright and full of people making noise. This, to them, was another sign of the world they knew disappearing. Alexis, Janice, and a few others did what they could to comfort the children as much as possible, but it wasn't the easiest thing when they needed comforting just as much.

Boone left the gymnasium by himself. He walked over to the door where they came in. He peered out the window, which was now lying in pieces on the floor mixed with Jon-Jon's blood, and noticed shadows moving in the distance. He took a deep breath and took twice as long to exhale. He had no idea what he was doing anymore. He used to have an idea about what to do, but it seemed no matter what he did people died. Their deaths, each and every one took a chunk out of his will and now he was left feeling uneasy and defeated. Going ahead wasn't a good idea, but there was no going back.

Outside, under the cloak of night, the school became a lighthouse to the undead vessels lost among the debris of a world in ruin. Somehow they knew, either by scent or noise, or some omniscient knowledge. The living dead knew that life was somewhere inside that building, and they wanted it. With hands stretching outward and stiff legged movements pulling them forward they moved closer.

For those who couldn't sleep, or needed something to do, there was a gathering outside the gymnasium. They got together anything that could be of immediate use. They sealed up the window Jon-Jon broke and began barricading any other weak spots they could find. They worked diligently as the others rested.

6 NO PLACE LIKE HOME

After the firefight at the roadblock all the boys in blue and their mish-mosh of friends and neighbors remained on edge. All with a multitude of different reasons, and some with no reason other than the obvious. There were too many questions with too little answers and nothing was making sense. There had easily been a hundred of those things descending upon their home, New Haven. They had every right to feel relief, yet they didn't feel it. Most of them were bewildered. Many of them thought that if they had been dead once before, what was to stop them from getting up after dying again. They had no reassurances. The best they could do was to put these dead things into such ill-repair that it would be impossible for them to move at all afterwards. Would these things stay dead now, they wondered? But no one knew.

Dead used to mean dead. No one knew what it meant anymore. No one knew if it would ever stop. No one knew if things would ever be normal again, or how many more of those things were walking to town now. No one knew anything.

To play it safe, Sheriff Davis had been instructing everyone to incinerate the bodies as best as possible. There had been no reports of the undead reanimating multiple times, but Davis wasn't going to give these things the chance to. In Davis's eyes the news was always bullshit, and biased bullshit at that, he didn't think there were any real journalists left on earth, but it would seem that they were at least partly right about recent events. The recently deceased were returning to life, in some sense of the word, though not all. The news had plenty of halfcocked ideas; a form of human rabies, mass psychosis, murder cults. The speculative fiction grew wilder from channel to channel. The only thing Davis and the plethora of news men and women agreed upon were the means of which to permanently dispatch the dearly departed; destroy the brain or incinerate the bodies. He'd been doing both with a mild sense of satisfaction since the first time he witnessed one of the deaders stumbling through town.

Plumes of dark velvety smoke filled the air. It blocked sight of the setting sun, and Davis's men were choking on it. The smell was unreal. It was a mix of barbecue, without the sweet, and week-old summer road kill. Ash clung to their skin and mingled with their sweat, turning it into a muddy second skin. The steady, smooth, feathery rainfall helped to peel it away, but not by much. They dragged the bodies of the dead closer together and set them to flame. The rain made it tougher, but they eventually took to it and burned up all the same. What was left of the dead looked like it crawled from out of the black top. Some of the bodies burned brighter than others, and when someone pointed it out Davis told them why.

"Women burn brighter, I heard. Something about a higher fat ratio."

Back at Walter's house, the kids were falling asleep upstairs as Maria stayed with them to make sure they did so quickly. Then the adults could talk freely without fear of terrifying their children further, though Jeff and his family did a good job at keeping them sheltered from what was really happening. The kids just thought that people were sick with a new kind of flu, and that they had to stay home and away from other people. They didn't mind it much, and loved not having to go to school, but occasionally they'd get stir crazy and bored. The soft sound of rain on the roof helped to muffle the noise from downstairs; the yawning, the tapping of hands, and the beginnings of conversations that would abruptly end as they waited for Maria. The radio hadn't come back on, and stations had been going on and off before (usually with notice). But this time it was without warning—just white noise and jittered scrambles. Walter suggested that they would take to the road and start broadcasting from a mobile unit.

Walter was known for his hope however, even in the worst of

situations. But his son was another story altogether.

Maria quietly crept down the stairs and into the family room.

"What did I miss?" Maria asked.

"Nothing really, just talking about the radio stations," Walter replied.

Maria snuggled up next to Jeff. She held him close and he reciprocated. The light rain was consistent, with no lightning or thunder at the moment.

"So do we sit here and wait?" Jeff asked.

"What else can we do?" Barbara asked.

"We're not going to any safe zones, and we're not going near the city. We're staying put unless we have no other choice but to leave, we've got everything we need right here," Walter grumped.

"No, definitely not, that's not an option," his son agreed.

"We have no communication with anyone outside of town. We have no idea what's really going on out there. There's no reason we should leave" Laura said.

"Agreed," said Maria.

"That's all well and good, but how long till we run out of food?" Walter asked.

"I'm more worried about the next few days. We can last at least two weeks till we need food. I want to know what the hell is going on out there that would make a dead man get up and walk," Jeff spewed. "What if these things show up here? We don't have many weapons. And what if it is a disease like some people are saying? I don't want to mess with that, I certainly don't want the kids exposed to it."

"We can go see Davis tomorrow. He's dealt with these things already. Maybe get a walkie-talkie, see what him and the boys are doing to keep everybody safe. Maybe they heard something. Maybe we can see what the deal is with the power," said Walter.

"We can't depend on them. They have to look out for themselves and their families. We should definitely talk to them…I just wish the news or the radio would come on and give us some the answers," Maria began to cry.

Jeff held her tightly "I know babe, I know."

"There's so much we don't know," Barbara said.

"We're in the dark on this one, literally. You should all get some sleep. I'll take first watch and when the sun comes up, Jeff and I will go see what Davis has to say," Walter stood up and walked toward the window nearest the front door. He was done with the conversation, and had said what he needed to say and that was that. They weren't leaving, so the only thing he needed to do now was keep them safe, and that meant keeping an eye on what was walking around outside. From what he could see there was nothing right now, but he knew it wouldn't stay that way, not for long anyway.

Nobody argued. Jeff walked Maria up the stairs to the guest room, Jeff's old room, which had now become the kids' room. Laura and Barbara both went to Walter's side. Laura held him and Barbara peeked out the windows with her arms crossed and a chill sitting firmly on her spine. Maria nudged her way onto the beds. Jeff kissed her and looked at his kids. He looked around the room, looked at the only boarded up window on the second floor, and then back to his kids. Maria and he locked eyes for a moment and then Jeff walked out of the room and back down the stairs.

Laura started toward the stairs as Jeff was halfway down them. She put her hand on the dark wood rail that would guide her to her room, only a few feet from Maria and the kids. Jeff said goodnight to his mother and made his way to his fathers' side, putting his arm around his sister.

Barbara was scared and felt alone. She had her family but lacked the intimacy that Jeff and Maria had with each other, or her parents for that matter. She had recently removed herself from a long-term relationship with her high school sweetheart that was going nowhere. She was finishing up her last year of college and looking forward to an engagement that never happened. She wondered if her ex was thinking as much about her as she was of him. At least she felt safe, that much she was sure of, if nothing else.

The three of them paced around for a bit and when Barbara grew tired she left them for the comforts of her bedroom, which she'd only slept in when she came home from school. She didn't take much of her old furniture to her dorm. Most of it was too bulky for the tiny shared living space. Seeing her old dresser took her back to simpler times, it still had her and her exes names carved in it and plenty of old stickers from bands she used to like back in high school.

7 BLOOD AND ASH

Morning came quickly for the Caulfields, and before Jeff could fully wake up, Walter stood over him. Jeff's eyes were partially sealed shut with crust and lack of sleep but after seeing his father hunched over him, he forced them to open. It reminded him of when he still lived with his parents and his father would wake him up early to go fishing on occasion down at Johnson's Lake. How he wished his father had a fishing pole in his hand. He did not, only the look of determination. He had something to do, and he planned on doing it.

He sat up and said, "I'll be down in a minute."

Fifteen minutes later Jeff groggily came down the stairs. Barbara and Laura were sitting with Walter at the kitchen table and smiled at the sorry site that was Jeff upon his arrival at the foot of the stairs. He smiled back, "you ready or what," he called to his father.

"Wise-ass, let's go," Walter said.

Next to the family van, which was loaded up in case they needed to leave, was Walter's pick up truck. It was old and dirty but more reliable than anything he had ever owned before or since. They climbed in and drove off. Jeff searched the radio dial for a station but found nothing but the sound of static. He kept it on in case something broke through the noise. Walter found it irritating but couldn't find a better reason to shut it off. They drove south on Mokar Street and headed into town.

The town was empty. A few cars remained parked in their usual spots and every storefront worth its window was boarded up and marked as 'closed till further notice'. Walter found this hilarious, as if the boarded up windows didn't sufficiently state that the store was not open. They made a left down Roosevelt Street and pulled up in front of the police station. There were rows of trucks and cars haphazardly parked all over the street. The vehicles smelled of burnt rubber and overcooked bacon and looked as if they mistakenly drove through a slaughterhouse instead of a carwash. There wasn't a spot on any of the vehicles that wasn't covered in blood and ash.

They entered the station and walked into a whirlwind of harried conversations and manic rantings. Upon the door opening, every wild-eyed man in the room swung their head to look in their direction. After they recognized Walter and his son, and realized they were of the living, breathing variety, they nodded and turned back to their ramblings. Walter searched the crowd for Sheriff Davis and found him heading directly toward them but looked like he might plow right through them. He was carrying his jacket in one hand and a cup of tea in the other.

"Really fucking busy right now," Davis said as he brushed past them.

"You heard anything, Bruce," Walter asked.

"You don't want to know what I've been hearing Walt. Crazy shit. End of the human race kind of shit," Davis said.

"Well," Jeff piped up.

"Well, besides the hell that was last night, I hear on the ham this morning that L.A. was bombed, probably terrorists, but who the fuck knows. Don't know if it was one bomb, car bombs, dirty bombs—as usual we're in the dark. But it's getting even darker, if someone's dropping nukes, shit—I don't even want to think about it!" Davis walked toward his truck.

"Shit," Walter said.

"Yeah, shit is right," Davis replied.

Davis started his beast of a truck and rode off as he left the two men dumbfounded on the side of the road. Their thoughts were heavier than wet sandbags on a baby's back. The city of angels was wing-clipped. As if dealing with dead folk who refused to die wasn't enough, now they had to think of the additional tragedies that were befalling the West coast and what if it was happening elsewhere. They were close enough to Titan City and New York City was only a stone's throw from there. If something were to happen it could have an effect on New Haven. Being a small town had its advantages but escaping big disasters wasn't necessarily one of them. They had family and friends in those cities.

Walter and Jeff solemnly walked back to the truck. The static didn't bother Walter at all this time—he was relieved to be hearing anything. They drove toward the North roadblock, slowly following behind Davis (Walter didn't exactly want to go back home just yet and felt if he lingered around Davis and his men he'd be able to get some more info out of them) and from a mile away they could smell nothing but acrid smoke. The smoke dug into their nostrils and planted roots. By the time they got to the actual roadblock they could see what made the smell. Hundreds of bodies lie strewn about in horrific poses. Their flesh and bone were charred black as tar. It looked as if the black top itself was giving birth to the most macabre of Halloween mannequins. Adjacent to the road were lines of cars. Most of the cars looked to have sale signs from George's Lot stuck to the windshields. Davis and his men set up a barricade of used but guaranteed to run steel.

They saw many familiar faces behind the vehicles, many of them taking aim on things that looked like people in the distance. They weren't people however, not anymore at least—they were dead, all messed up and moving forward.

A whistling noise was heard in the air, faint but fast. Those that heard it looked to the northern sky. They couldn't see anything at first, but then a noise was heard and a gigantic plume of smoke and debris rose into the air. The smoke rose as high as the distant skyline and then further still. The city of angels would not be the only city to fall today. Titan City now lay wasted as well. A titan turned to ash, and the ash only a fading memory.

As they stood and stared, in something worse than disbelief, another noise was heard in the distance. A moment later, in proximity to the first tower of debris, rose another. It was twice as devastating. The world never seemed so bleak—so punished, so doomed. It could've been New York City, Jersey City, or Liberty City—any other city close by for that matter. Alan, a good friend of many of the men there, had turned his gun to himself without drawing any attention till it was too late. They all stared at the magnificent destruction in the distance. He opened his mouth, letting his teeth scrape against the cold metal. Alan was but one breath away from oblivion.

They stared at the massive clouds of burning debris that disintegrated into ash as the mushroom shaped cloud continued to form. Alan didn't look at any of his friends. He closed his eyes as the plumes of smoke rose higher. Not a single tear rolled down his cheek. He leaned up against a car, his back to the fallen Titan, bit down on the barrel, cracking and chipping his teeth as he awkwardly pulled the trigger. The skyline was erased. A single shot rang out in the immediate area and those that weren't too stunned to look immediately regretted having done so. The noise barely registered. His head slumped forward with the barrel of his rifle lodged in his mouth. The back of his head was blown out across a white Toyota Camry. Some of his friends noticed it then. Disgusted, heartbroken, Davis stared at his friend.

Less than a minute after the gunshot, Alan twitched. His body spasmed and he lifted up his head. His dead eyes gazed upon his friends. Davis stared into those dead eyes with eyes as equally empty. Alan reached up and murmured some sort of noise, "sssshhhlsssseeeelllf." He sounded like a snake but Davis shot him dead a second time before he could bite. Jeff vomited. No one was able to well up enough tears to cry—it seemed they were dried up of emotion at the moment. All they could do was stare into the billowing clouds of smoke, and at what remained of their friend. Davis shed a tear for those who couldn't and quickly wiped it away— it may have been the last one he had left.

The ham radios crackled with frantic voices but no one listened to what they were saying. The only hope they had was that the bombs weren't atomic. The nuclear fallout resulting from three bombs would be a global concern. Radiated debris could travel great lengths by way of the wind, possibly contaminating food and water supplies. Fallout shelters are rarely maintained, a few might still be functional due to the increase of terror threats in recent years, but on the whole, fallout shelters have just become additional storage space for the buildings that house them. They are hardly more than a relic leftover from the cold war, one that New Haven certainly didn't maintain. They had one at the church, and one at the school.

Laura greeted Walter and her son at the door upon their return home. She could tell immediately that something serious was weighing down on their shoulders. Walter kissed her and held her close. He walked her outside and pointed to the North. She began to cry. Maria and Barbara were playing with the children. Once the kids saw their father walk through the door Wally, Sandra, and Tommy ran to him. His solemn expression broke and a smile emerged as he knelt to the ground and opened his arms wide. His smile was sincere but it only served to hide what he was thinking on the inside.

"Daddy," the kids screamed, as he wrapped his arms around them.

Maria too, could tell something was off. Once Jeff knelt down she could see beyond him through the picturesque silhouette of the doorframe and saw her in-laws wrapped in each other's quivering arms. She walked over to Jeff, and Barbara followed behind her. Maria looked to Jeff for an explanation but he refused to give one in front of the children, not that they would be able to grasp the ramifications anyway. Barbara pulled Maria by the arm and the two of them joined Walter and Laura outside. They too looked to the North, but neither of them was prepared to see the giant mushroom clouds dissipating into the grey sky.

Jeff refused to move away from his kids. He sat and watched them play. He buried his feelings deep inside and hoped they'd be obedient enough to stay there. He began to tremble. If only he could put time on hold and live in a moment. All he wanted was to keep his family safe, but how could he protect them now? He chewed on the thought, but all he ended up with was a mouthful of blood and chewed up lip.

8 SIEGE

From the shadows emerged a veritable swarm of the undead. In all the varying degrees of rot, they moved forth. Moving in an almost tidal fashion, swaying side to side, back and forth, they staggered closer. They verbalized their hunger for warm living flesh with guttural sounds and slurring hisses that could almost be words. In the horde of creatures were all walks of former life; death did not spare the young, the elderly, the rich, the beautiful, the crippled, or the undecided. They all marched forward in need. Their pride or shame died when they came back, leaving only hunger.

Inside the school, Jon-Jon, weak from blood loss and general exhaustion, refused to rest. As far as he was concerned he'd sleep when he was dead, so long as someone was kind enough to destroy his undead brain. He, as well as many others, was doing a fair job of barricading the building. The building itself was as strong as they came; it was the windows that worried them. Luckily, they sat high in relation to a person's height and, as in most schools, they were shatterproof. Though shatterproof was a relative term and a barrage of blunt force would prove it so; tenacious, unending blunt force at that. These things didn't stop unless they were stopped, and barricading themselves in was the first in a long list of things to do to stop them, at least enough of them, in order to survive another day, another hour, or just for another minute.

Gerty sat on a toilet seat in the woman's rest room. She took deep, painfully sharp breaths as she clutched her chest. She had a metal shard sticking out of her skin, and by the way it felt she knew it had pierced her lung. She wasn't sure how bad it was, she'd been running on adrenaline for the last few hours and only began feeling the pain sometime during the drive down route 519. Her shirt was soaked with blood, but she was able to remedy that, at least.

She pulled a tube of crazy glue from her bag, a nearly exhausted roll of duct tape, and a winged sanitary pad. She always kept Krazy Glue on hand to fix her key chains. Gerty had an impressive amount of key chains, and they always seemed to break.

They were usually keepsakes from vacations or gifts from friends, who went on vacation and brought them back for her. She tended to crack them and break them often given that they usually were not of the greatest quality. But regardless of quality they held tremendous value to her. She'd rather glue them than discard them. They were her memories and it was better to have broken memories than none at all.

Once she saw the wound, she immediately thought of a story she heard about Krazy Glue; that it had been invented as a suture-less solution for field surgery in the Vietnam War. She wasn't entirely certain on the validity of the story but knew that it could be used as a skin-glue. She didn't have many options and feared going to the group for help. If they thought she could become one of those things, someone might just kill her on the spot. Or they may leave her behind as well. Either way there wasn't much any of them could do for her anyway. She didn't think it was worth the risk. If the glue didn't work she'd always have the option to ask for help anyway.

Gerty bit her lip and pulled out the metal shard. The pain hit her, and she watched as bright blood streamed from the wound. Her skin color grew pale quickly as she ripped open the sanitary pad and pressed it firmly to her wound. She held it there tightly as she watched it fill with blood. She began to cough and wheeze as her lungs took in some of the vital fluid.

After about two minutes of keeping pressure on it, she pulled the pad away from the top of the wound just enough to fill it with some glue. The blood had stopped oozing but if she released the pressure too much the floodgates would surely open. She carefully began gluing the ends of her flesh back together, making sure to put glue inside the wound as well, no matter how painful it was. She used a lot of her supply of glue, and after a moment she put the pad back on full force.

She waited a good long while before she moved the pad again. Eventually she removed it, and duct taped a fresh pad to her chest before returning to the gymnasium to rest. She had lost a lot of blood, and feared the damage to her lung may be mortal. Her cough had worsened—a sure sign of fluid in the lung. She went to sleep.

The dead things had reached the building. Their cold fingers clamored at the brick exterior, feeling for a way in. They soon swarmed the front of the school in layers three, four, and sometimes five deep; all lurching forward to get inside. Some of them reached for the windows but none with any strength to shatter them just yet. There were so many of them, and so many of them unique in their grotesque appearances. One in particular had most of its face chewed off, so much so that its skull was more prevalent than what was left of its face. Another had her innards dragging behind her and splinters of bone coming through her leg and chest, as if she'd been hit by a truck.

There were cops, and firefighters, paramedics, and other emergency responders—even a National Guard member, whose uniform was so badly shredded he might as well be naked. None of them were pretty: they all had wounds, some more gaping than others. They came in droves, seemingly out of nowhere, backlit by the stars and moon casting their shadows towards the school.

Ben had walked away from the others. He went outside to the fenced in area behind the school. The creatures had made their way there as well, and their dead fingers wrapped around the chain links of the fence like eagle talons grasping their helpless prey. The fence wouldn't hold forever, he thought, but walked up to it anyway. He could tell it excited the dead things. From his pocket he pulled out a knife. He stood directly next to the fence, close enough so that the dead things could almost touch him, and he could smell their rot oozing off like dew on the morning grass. He smiled a twisted smile and jabbed the dead things with his knife. He stabbed at their faces, fingers, and anything else he could reach. He relished at the thought of catching an eye with the knife, maybe he'd even be able to pluck one out.

As he performed his wretched little version of Whack-A-Mole, he noticed on the overhang in the back of the building there was an access ladder leading up to the roof. He feverishly stabbed at the things as they continued to react to his presence. And when he felt contented he wiped the blood from his knife and walked back inside.

Ben rejoined the others. "Found a way to get to the roof," he announced.

Some people looked excited at the news, others seemed unimpressed. Most just wanted to get some rest.

"That's awesome! We can go up there and pick off the troublemakers when we finish this up," Boone said, getting up from the floor, leaving Sarah and Mila to themselves.

"Sounds good," Ben replied, licking his lower lip.

Eddie and Joseph sat on the floor next to their mother, Janice. They were the shattered remains of a family. Janice looked like she crawled out from the pits of hell. Her face was mostly expressionless but she perked up when her sons sat next to her. She tried to smile but it was almost as if it hurt her face to do so. She was paper-thin, the desire to eat had left her and anytime she tried to eat, more often than not, she threw it back up. She no longer cared to live. She didn't exactly want to die, but life had lost its luster for her. She only wanted to do what she could for her remaining children and if that meant surviving, then that's what she would try her hardest to do. The three of them had been through a lot, but Janice was the one who witnessed it all first hand. She was the one who watched her husband being eaten alive by a swarm of the undead bastards as they invaded their home. His last words to her were garbled and intermixed with bloodcurdling screams between every other syllable. But somehow she understood him: get the kids and go, I love you.

But she couldn't get the kids: Lizzie and Shaun were upstairs and the stairway was blocked by the mayhem she was witnessing. She ran outside and screamed up to the window, calling to them. The kids came running to the window, but they were being chased by one of the shambling dead things that had managed to make it upstairs into their room. She screamed for them to jump, but they were too afraid. She screamed so loud it hurt her teeth, and Shaun jumped to her but not before the creature had bitten his throat out. He died in her arms as she watched her only daughter get eviscerated on the windowsill.

When Shaun came back to life it was in her arms. He moaned for her warm flesh. She dropped him and stepped away, only to fall to her knees sobbing. Shaun came at her quickly; the fresh dead were quicker at first, though they eventually slowed down. It was then that Eddie and Joseph had returned from trying to get their grandmother, which had failed miserably—she'd been dead long before they arrived.

They returned home to see their youngest brother lurching after their hysterical mother. She screamed unintelligibly, and one could see why—how could you put what she was seeing into anything that made sense? They grabbed her and pulled her to the car as their father stumbled from the front doorway; his eyes and throat were missing and replaced with red pulps of flesh. They drove off then to Frankie's house, only a few streets away where a similar scene awaited them.

"What the fuck is happening?" Joseph screamed.

No one had an answer. Eddie tried to follow the road as his eyes swelled with tears, and Janice trembled hysterically in the back as she stared out the window at the dead pieces of her heart.

Eddie, Joseph, and Janice sat together for a bit, not saying much of anything and trying not to break down and cry. They couldn't, not now. There was simply no time for it. They had to survive.

Jon-Jon found Dawn sitting next to Ricker, and if Ricker wasn't so damn old and ugly he'd be worried that they had something going on. Not that Jon-Jon and Dawn had anything going on, but that didn't mean they weren't striving towards something, however subtle. Something was going on there. They both had lost someone, everybody lost someone, but they found something in the other that comforted them, and that was all they needed for the time being.

That's all anybody needed to keep them going.

9 ONE BAD APPLE SPOILS THE BARREL

From the roof of the school Boone peered out over the edge, looking down at the dead things that reached up. Near him were Damian, Ben, and Alexis, who also peered over the edge. Alexis was biting her fingernails nervously and cracking her neck. Ben was nearly expressionless and Damian was disgusted and angered. The smell was overpowering and if it hadn't been for a slight breeze it would've been downright unbearable.

Damian moved over to the far side of the roof and stood on the edge. He unzipped his pants, pulled out his member and urinated on the creatures below. He shifted from side to side making sure to spread his piss to as many of those things below as he could. Boone looked over and laughed and Ben snickered as well.

Alexis didn't even notice; her attention was focused on the creatures coming in the distance. She shivered and headed back downstairs. So many in such a short time, she thought. The three men stayed on the roof taking it all in, and gagging on the stench.

"Fuck, man, what're we supposed to do?" asked Damian.

"Nothing much we can do," Boone said tiredly. He was weary of being the appointed leader. He didn't know what to say anymore. He was tired and just wanted to be sleeping in his bed with the covers pulled up over his head and the blinds drawn shut.

"Not if they keep coming like this. I can't figure out why there's so many of them, and why do they seem to be drawn to us?" Ben added.

"Fucked if I know, man," Damian added as he looked out at the night.

"I say we stick around here as long as we can, maybe we can wait them out, maybe they'll move one?" Boone didn't sound as if he could convince even himself.

"If they moved on, we wouldn't be here." Ben grunted. "I'd say that's the damn problem."

"Fuck this, I'm gonna go to the kitchen and get me something to eat. If y'all get sick of staring at these freaks feel free to join me. Chef D's gonna whip something up." Damian then laughed as he made his way to the other end of the roof.

"Doesn't sound like a bad idea," Ben said, "could always go for another cup of coffee. I'll be down in a few."

Boone returned to staring at the creatures, hoping to find something in their eyes that made sense. But before he could find any answers, he felt the cold sharp pain of a knife being violently forced just left of his spine. Ben wrapped his hand around Boone's mouth as he twisted the knife and pulled it out only to repeat the act a few more times before taking his weapon and shoving him off the roof.

If the creatures could rejoice, they would have. Instead they pulled the warm flesh from Boone's body and moments later he stood as one of the dead.

Ben joined Damian in the cafeteria for a snack and some coffee. Chef D made a sizable stack of French toast for the two of them. The smell must have traveled to the gymnasium, because Frankie and a few others came to see who was cooking what and where the rest of it was.

"That other fool still on the roof, huh?"

"Yeah, said he was hungry though. He'll probably come down once he smell's these though," Ben laughed.

Once Ben had his fill he left the cafeteria and wandered around the dark and nearly empty school. He ran his fingers along the lockers, and looked into the empty rooms. He stopped for a drink at the water fountain, and then headed for the gymnasium to get some rest.

There he found an empty corner of the room and sat down. He rubbed his temples, and then his eyes. When he looked at his hands he could still see some of Boone's dried blood.

He looked to the farthest object from him and focused on it, he then repeated this exercise on the people in the room. He started with the left hand side, moving toward the right. He wasn't so much sizing everybody up as he was categorizing them. Ben loved to look at someone and then label them. It was something he began doing when he was very young, and had kept repeating throughout his life. He especially loved doing this at stores, watching what people bought, how they dressed, how quickly they walked. The quicker he could label a person, the more disposable they were; the harder to categorize, the more dangerous they were. Boone was easy; the leader. Shorty was his mask, a companion by shared disaster as it were, a way that he could seem less threatening to a group. People were hesitant of loners. Shorty was many things to Ben, therefore Shorty ended up in the miscellaneous section, were he would remain until further scrutiny. Scott and Judy could be summed up as lovers, but that was too easy. Strange would be a better fit, but they both had layers beyond that, either way they were too dangerous. Jon-Jon was simple, but was one of the reasons Ben was still alive now, so he got a free pass. Ricker was annoying, but he was constantly with Dawn. Dawn was thrown into the weak category, but being that it seemed she and Jon-Jon had something going on, she got a pass by association.

He kept playing his little mind games, and he was so enthralled with it that when Shorty came to sit by him it took Shorty snapping his fingers in his face for Ben to notice. Ben put his mind game aside so he could put his mask on. He made small talk with his friend, Shorty the mask. But he had an image in the back of his mind of a face he wanted to erase in the second-in-command category, a dangerous choice.

Dangerous as it might be, Ben just had a thing against authority. It was the one category he hated more than anything.

10 CAN'T ALWAYS GET WHAT YOU WANT

Two women from the group, Mila and Sarah, left the gymnasium. They had rested, even managing to sleep a few hours. The two of them groggily walked the halls of the school, which were being patrolled by Eddie, Frankie, Joseph, Alexis, Shorty, Ben, Damian, and a few others. Mila and Sarah began asking around for Boone. They had become friends with him during their journey.

The three of them had met while escaping their local hospital during the first few days of this would-be apocalypse. Days later they joined up with Jon-Jon, which later merged with Eddie's group. And now here they were. They walked toward the cafeteria after Damian had mentioned that he might be in there. Ben overheard him and began to make his way there via an alternate path, hurrying his pace once he rounded the corner and was out of site.

Mila and Sarah looked around the cafeteria, but it was empty except for the scent of syrup. Ben came in behind them.

"Hey," he said, "guess everybody left eh?"

"Oh, heh, yeah I guess so," said Sarah.

"Have you seen Boone around?" Mila asked.

"Last time I seen him we were on the roof," Ben replied. "I can take you up there. Maybe he's still there."

"Sure," Mila replied. Sarah also nodded in agreement.

Ben climbed the rungs of the ladder to the roof, with Mila and Sarah behind him. He walked them over to where Boone's last breath had been. He hadn't planned on doing anything to the girls but once they were up there and all alone, he couldn't help but play his mind game.

The only ties the two women had were to Boone, and they were the only ones who seemed concerned to where he was. With them out of the way too, Ben thought for sure no one would go around looking for him.

They were only tied to a man they didn't yet know was dead. No one would miss them. They fit into plenty of Ben's categories, and certainly weren't dangerous. If he could put just one label on them it would be toys. And Ben loved to play with his toys, especially now with all the time the end of the world afforded him to do so.

"Well, he was up here earlier, maybe he's in the bathroom," Ben chuckled.

"Okay, well, thanks. I guess we'll just go back down," Mila replied. "If you see him let him know we're looking for him."

"Sure, sure, no problem. Hey, before you two go back down come take a look at this. There's so many of them things, it's crazy," Ben said insistently.

The two women walked over to the edge of the building next to Ben. He watched their faces as they scanned the crowd of dead people. He hung on their every reaction, and waited for the one he was hoping to see. Sarah was the first to notice; her expression was of confusion and then dawning horror. She grabbed Mila's arm and pointed to the dead Boone below them. Mila's expression mirrored Sarah's and as they turned to look at Ben he plunged the knife into Mila's throat. She grasped at the knife, her eyes wide and unbelieving. Her feet fumbled backward and Ben kicked her in the stomach forcing her over the side as he wrapped his hand around Sarah's mouth to gag her screams.

Mila fell over the edge. For a moment it looked like she was crowd surfing at a metal concert, but the hands that would ordinarily keep her afloat and grope at her feminine qualities instead only pulled her down. She writhed in pain, kicking and screaming as the creatures pulled her to the damp earth. The last face she saw was Boone's, right before he took a bite out of her's. Luckily for her, the knife wound bled her out before the dead could tear her apart. Soon enough she would rise as one of them, and wouldn't even bother with removing the knife.

Sarah struggled to break free from Ben's grip. But so did many other women before her, and none of them were ever successful…

save his earliest work.

So, when Sarah did break free it was a huge shock to Ben, and also exhilarating. She kicked him and stomped him, bit at his fingers and squirmed. But it was a combination of the squirming, the stomping, and the shifting of her weight and a well-placed elbow to the side of the face that knocked Ben to the side.

It wasn't much, but it was enough to get free of him and put some distance between them. She screamed for help as loud as she could, as she continued to back away from the crazy eyed man that had killed her only two friends she had left on this earth. As her heart filled with rage she realized her screams were not saving her. That rage, however, was turning into something. She could feel it rising up inside her, like boiling water spilling out of pot.

Sarah charged at her attacker, with eyes as fierce and unforgiving as his. She tackled him to the ground and wailed her fists into him. Ben, caught completely off guard by her assault, could do little to avoid her. She pummeled him repeatedly, breaking the skin of her knuckles on his face and teeth. Ben did what he could do to block her, but she was too fast in her fury and high on adrenaline.

Ben managed to roll off his back and onto his side as he shoved her off, landing a hateful right hook to the side of her face. She bled on impact and staggered to the side but quickly got to her feet. The two of them faced each other again, back in the same situation but all the worse for the wear.

"You got some fire, sweetheart, I'll give you that. But we're just having a little fun," Ben smiled.

"Go to hell," she screamed.

"This…IS…hell, bitch, and I'm the devil!" Then he smiled wider.

"You ain't shit! You're just a sick fuck!" she snarled back at him. "And when everybody finds out what you did, you'll be a DEAD sick fuck!"

"Like I said, this is just for fun. I was hoping for a little something more, but I can see you're really not all that into me. Give your little lady friend a kiss from me," he told her as he pulled a gun from his waistband.

He raised the gun and aimed it at her but before he could squeeze the trigger she ran to the edge of the roof and jumped off. Ben ran to the edge as well and watched her land just past the rows of dead folk. She twisted her ankle as she hit the ground, but kept moving.

Ben aimed at her again and fired. The bullet grazed her arm, but she kept running, letting out only the mildest of whimpers. Ben fired again but only wasted the bullet. She disappeared into the night.

As Ben turned around Frankie appeared behind him and cracked him in the face with the butt of his shotgun. Ben was knocked out cold, falling to the ground hard. Eddie, Damian, and Chung-Hee rolled him over and searched him for any other weapons, but found none. A few others made their way to the roof to see what all the commotion was about.

"I knew something was off with him the moment I saw him," Chung-Hee said.

"What the fuck do we do with him now?" Damian asked.

"Fucked if I know," Eddie replied.

"I got an idea," Chung-Hee said, looking hesitant to share his thoughts, but thinking it might just give them the chance to get out of the school while they still had the chance to.

11 THE DEAD COME SLOWLY, BUT STEADY AS THE MORNING SUN

After Jeff and Walter told their loved ones what they saw, and what had happened with Sheriff Davis' friend Alan, it was as if they had been stricken numb with silence. The daylight lit the inside of the house a hazy orange. The skies outside grew grey, not like the grey of a storm coming, but more like the blue in the sky died kind of grey.

The kids were kept comfortably in the dark on the topic of citywide destruction. They knew of the walking dead but their exposure to it was minimal. They usually only grew scared come night: during the day it was just difficult to keep them inside. They played in the house, kids on parade, with little metal cars and plastic men.

Their adventures were grand, and their imaginations ran wild. They turned their room into one giant fort, and were in the midst of creating more around the house. The adults just sat staring at the walls, as if they would burst into flames and be nothing more than dust. They wished they could be kids, where the biggest worry would be how to make the next fort.

Walter wondered what kind of bomb it could have been. Nuclear was on the top of his list. Considering the explosion and cloud appearance he was guessing it could've been an atomic bomb, or hydrogen bomb. Though Walter wasn't familiar with biological or chemical warfare, he also thought those were possibilities as well. And with modern warfare going the way it was couldn't they devise a weapon capable of doing both?

Walter's mind swirled out of control and he was no better off for trying to figure out what type of bomb he had witnessed exploding. There was also the possibility of it being an entirely new type of bomb. After all, man loved finding new ways to kill.

Jeff pulled himself off the couch, which was no easy task, and sat closer to the kids. He watched them play, wishing he could do the same. He felt it coming and tried as hard as he could to keep it down: but once the first tear forced its way out of his eye the rest came running. No matter how much he tried to fight each tear he had rivers running down the sides of his tired face. All those buried feelings had finally crawled their way to the top.

"What's wrong daddy?" asked his little princess, Sandra.

"Nothing baby," he lied. "Daddy's just sad."

Everyone turned to look as they heard Jeff's quavering voice. His eyes red and wet, he couldn't look at them. His sons, Wally and Tommy came over to him, and Maria went to join him as well. It wasn't long after that, when everyone began to cry.

"I…just want you to know that daddy loves you kids so much, okay. No matter what happens, I love you. I love all of you, Dad, Ma, Barb." He wrapped his arm around his wife. "I love you babe." Then he broke down and sobbed in Maria's arms.

His kids told him how much they loved him too, wrapping their arms around his legs. His parents and sister also expressed their love as they tried to fight back their own tears. Walter didn't cry though. he couldn't allow it—he had to remain strong. His throat dried up and his eyes itched. He wanted to let himself go, but he gripped his nerves and refused to give in to them.

***

On the other side of town, in Susie's apartment, which he affectionately called the Kemp Estate, Dane washed vigorously. He had blood and bits of gore all over his body, even chunks of it stuck in his hair. He took a rag to his nails, and scrubbed them till they nearly bled.

Susan sat on the lid of the toilet, as pale as the porcelain below her, staring at Dane's blood covered uniform.

"What are we going to do?" She cried.

"We're going to do nothing," Dane replied in a voice as monotone as a robot.

"What? But why? We have to do something don't we?" she pleaded.

"I've done all I can right now. I haven't slept in days. When I'm done washing this shit off I'm going to lie down on the bed and hold you till I fall asleep. And when I wake up this nightmare will be over and I'll be back to handing out speeding tickets and breaking up parties under the trestle."

"Yeah, so I should just go open the deli and turn on the grill right?" Susan quipped. "Cause when you wake up the world is gonna be right back to fucking normal." She shook her head and walked out of the bathroom.

Dane had a funny comeback but decided to keep it to himself. He only had a few hours before he had to report back to the roadblock and didn't want to waste them fighting and then apologizing.

He turned off the water and grabbed his towel off the rack. He gave himself a once over with it and walked out of the room and into the bedroom where Susan was holding her face in her hands and crying on the bed. Dane wrapped the towel around his waist and sat by her side.

Shortly after, Cher, their old mutt of a dog trotted in and jumped on the bed next to them, nuzzling her way in between them. Susan rustled Cher's head and ears while wiping away her own tears.

Dane smiled at her and asked, "Do you want to lie down for a while?"

"Sure, but don't expect me to fall asleep or do anything else," she said.

"Fair enough," Dane said as he put his head on his pillow and closed his eyes. "I'm too tired to do anything anyway—it would just be embarrassing."

"Isn't it always," she joked, giving him a sly smile.

The three of them lay on the bed, spooning one another. Dane fell asleep almost instantly, and despite her declaration otherwise Susan joined him shortly after that. Cher slept with one eye open, ever the watchful guard dog.

Sal and Jones finished their shift, having only fired a few rounds. There had been a dozen or so lurkers approaching town and despite the events of late it had been an easy few hours. Their replacements were Keith, a fellow officer, and Henry, an avid hunter who was probably a better rifleman than the rest of them.

Keith reeked of whiskey, but no one said anything. And who could blame him. He had a drinking problem years ago but went cold sober of his own accord and never faltered. They exchanged handshakes with one another and parted ways.

Immediately they took to surveying the area with the scopes of their rifles. There were plenty of targets, slow and spread out. They cleared the area in a few minutes, and Keith went over to his truck to fetch himself another drink. He had a little more than half a bottle of Jack Daniels. He took a swig and offered some to Henry who wasn't foolish enough to turn it down even if he did hate Jack.

Sheriff Bruce Davis was patrolling the town, driving through the areas of town that were blind spots to the roadblocks. He'd dispatched a few of the dead things he came across by his lonesome. He also went around at random, checking on the townspeople, making sure those who stuck around were doing as well as they could. He did his best to avoid lengthy conversations, but he wanted people to be at ease. So if getting his ear chewed off was what he had to do, he'd do it for them.

During his drive he came across a dead thing that had made it half way through town. It made him wish he could build a fence around the whole town: barbed wire, spotlights, and guard decks. And the works, and why not, it was his wish.

He drove past Alan's house and since he was in the mood for wishing, he wished his friend didn't just off himself. Alan hadn't been taking anything well lately. His mother died last summer, who was the only family he had. And a few months ago his cat died, which he loved just as much. He hadn't had a steady woman in over two years, and the last time he tried talking to one, the woman's husband punched him in the mouth.

He was also in debt up to his ears. Which was no big thing if you asked around, but he made it a big thing. Then he nearly lost his mind when the dead started trying to eat people, as did everybody else. But he really took it badly, from the moment he heard word of it. He thought God was mad. And if he was, he had every right to be. Bruce wished his friend was riding along with him right now. But wishing never seemed to work, so he kept on driving.

***

Walter continued to play out all the scenarios in his head, and it was quickly getting clustered. He eventually decided that if it was a nuclear attack, then surely there would be nuclear fallout to follow. He remembered reading up on what to do in case of fallout years ago, and only now did what little information he could recall seem useful.

The first priorities were food and water. Food they had plenty, water they had some. But he remembered reading that any empty container should be filled, and used before any bottled water. He rose to his feet, quite excitedly, and began giving out duties for everyone. He instructed everyone to find any bottles or jars and fill them with water, any pots or pans as well. He ran to the bathroom, and turned on the faucet to the sink and tub, to fill them.

Walter instructed Jeff to go around and seal up all the windows so that no fallout dust could get inside. Walter then ran down to the basement, fetching a plastic tarp and a roll of duct tape, with it he sealed up the fireplace. Once all of the empty containers were filled with water they were brought to the basement.

After that everybody helped to move the seating furniture directly in the center of the room as best as possible. Walter remembered that the more distance there was between you and the radiation outside, the better off you were. He recalled that with every passing hour the radiation weakened. He didn't, however, recall how long it took for the radiation to be harmless. He knew it could take years and remembered something called half-life, but didn't remember much about it. They were far enough away that the larger quantities of dust wouldn't be an issue, but if the wind blew it in the direction of New Haven they'd have to worry all the same. It might not ever come to New Haven but Walter wasn't about to bet on it, nor anyone else in the family. They agreed to stay indoors for a few days, and only go out if they had to leave for an emergency, or to ward off the random dead.

Thinking of the dead gave Walter a horrible thought. The kind of thought that took the wind right from his sails—the dead would be perfect carriers of radiation. His mind spun out of control and hit a telephone pole. He sat back down, again at a loss for words. His family could tell something bothered him, and they could tell that he was keeping it to himself, like a hungry dog chewing on a bone.

Barbara looked out the window and gasped. Three dead things were coming toward the house, and they didn't look like they wanted to borrow a cup of sugar. She continued to watch, and was happy to see the Sheriff show up. He pulled his car to the side of them, got out with his handgun drawn. He walked up to them and put two bullets in each of their heads at point blank range. It was enough to keep them down till he could send someone out to burn them up.

Barbara didn't smile. She was relieved he did what he did. But she was disgusted by the brutal manner in which he did it.

12 SCHOOL'S OUT FOREVER

Chung-Hee searched through the school for rope or something strong enough to bind Ben. He had discussed his plan with those on the roof who witnessed his actions as well as Shorty who wasn't there at the time. He objected to Chung-Hee's plan but didn't have a better one. And, anyway, the majority sided with Chung-Hee, and during the end of the world the majority rules.

Uncertain of when to carry out this plan, they held an impromptu meeting in the gymnasium. Everyone was gathered, and no one was left to keep watch, though they did quickly check and make sure the place wasn't being infiltrated.

Eddie spoke loudly. "Everybody listen up, please. We have some terrible news and a tough decision to make."

"What do you mean? What's wrong?" a number of people asked in the crowd.

"If you'll let me talk, you'll know everything," Eddie replied to them. He paused, waiting for a silent confirmation. When he got it he continued. "Boone and his friend Milah were murdered by this man." He pointed to Ben, who was lying bound on the ground under Chung-Hee's foot.

Everyone gasped. Some of them began to cry while others proclaimed their newly found hatred for Ben. Shorty, though, just felt shame, and took a step back.

"We have a suitable punishment in mind for this bastard. But it's going to depend on us leaving. Which is the reason why we're having this meeting. We need to decide whether to stay or to go. As most of you probably know, we are surrounded. We can still access our vehicles. But if we wait much longer we may have to leave them behind." He paused, letting that sink in, before continuing. "And if we wait too long we may never be able to leave this place."

"How many are there?" Ricker asked.

"Maybe a hundred," Frankie answered.

"There are more and more by the hour. Most of our weapons are outside in the vehicles. Maybe, if we had them, staying wouldn't be a bad idea," Eddie postulated. "There's plenty of food and space, and the building is ideal. But we can't punch these things to death. I think it's best if we leave now. What do you all want to do?" Eddie asked.

The majority ruled once again. It was time to leave and head back to the road. Not everybody was happy with the decision, but no one knew what else to do. It would be too dangerous to try getting to the cars and back: that was a one way street.

Chung-Hee and Eddie explained the plan. While some would've said Ben's punishment was cruel, this was a cruel world, and always had been. The façade of pleasantries and complacency died when the dead rose, and the animal side of man that lay dormant for so long now stepped in without hesitation.

Ben was a killer, and if he remained free then he would kill again. There was nothing left for him to do on this world but die a slow painful death like all the ones he'd bestowed onto others. With his punishment, he would finally be able to give back and not just take. His death would let others live.

Eddie regretted the leadership position thrust upon him by the untimely demise of Boone, but just as Boone fell into it so did Eddie. After the meeting people came to him, wanting answers for which he had none. And they wanted something to do, which he was more than happy to give them.

Damian, Jon-Jon, and Joseph gathered the others by the front doors. Scott and Judy stayed near the door where they had initially broken in, waiting for a signal from Julio and the tall man, Corey. Julio and Corey were waiting for the signal from Chung-Hee, Eddie and Shorty, who were tying Ben to the fence outside.

Their intention was to use him as bait once they opened the fence to let the dead things in. Ben tried to struggle and break free. But every time he did, one of them would hit him hard to take the fight out of him just long enough to finish tying him up. Once he was tied up they ran to the fence opening closest to the building and started to make some noise.

They readied themselves as Eddie opened the fence, still hollering and yelling at the dead. "Dinner's ready motherfuckers!" Chung-Hee ran to the cafeteria and Eddie followed behind just as the dead things began to creep inside the area.

But Shorty hesitated.

"They're just going to chase us. They won't even know Ben is out there!" Shorty yelled. "I'm going to lead them to him. Go!"

"Wait! What about you?" Eddie asked.

"I'll get there. Just wait for me," he yelled over the moans of the oncoming dead.

Shorty back stepped toward Ben, yelling at the dead things in order to pull them further into the fenced in field. In one hand he held his crowbar, and in the other his handgun. He raised his gun to fire and took aim to the head of the dead thing closest to him. It was a gruesome looking thing, full of tear marks and gouged flesh. Its eyes were bulged and nose nearly gone. He would've been naked if it weren't for his underwear and lonesome sock. Shorty fired, and the thing dropped. The noise shattered the night, an owl cooed, and a familiar voice whispered something into Shorty's ear as a knife plunged into the lower right side of his back. Shorty turned around to see Ben and his bloodied face smiling.

"That's what you get for letting the gook tie me up. I thought we were friends, man," Ben smiled, his face swollen.

"H…how…," Shorty grunted.

"Fuckin' magic is how. I've been hiding knives since I could hold one."

Shorty dropped to his knees clutching at his back. Ben stepped closer and snatched his gun and crowbar. Then he kicked Shorty onto his back, driving the blade deeper. Shorty screamed. The dead things swarmed over him. Ben stepped back to watch for a bit, amazed at how fierce the dead things were. And how hungry.

"Looks like your plan is still going to work, eh?" Ben laughed. "Wish things could've been different, you were all right in my book," Ben shook his head.

The front doors of the school burst open. It was like the last day of class as everyone ran for their vehicles. Eddie, Frankie, Jon-Jon, and Joseph made sure everyone got out of the building and safely into a vehicle. Cars and trucks started at random, and some prematurely drove away with no destination other than the road. A safe zone was a pipe dream and they'd settle for a mall if they came across one.

Eddie looked from the vehicles back to the school, wondering if they could make it back. There was still thirty or forty of those things near the front and more coming from behind and to the side. It was too risky, but was it riskier to get back on the road, he wondered.

Ben began working his way through the flesh-eating creatures, knocking them down and out of the way so he could get to the roof access. It was impossible for him to reach the door to the school, and he was in no shape to climb the fence and face what wait in the darkness, so he figured it was the next best thing. His captors may have not done the best job tying him up or checking him, but they did a good job at beating the hell out of him.

As the convoy waited for Shorty, some of the dead creatures from the front saw the convoy and began moving in their direction. Ben had made it to the roof and was surprised to see how well the plan had come together. He laughed with wholehearted sincerity, then raised his gun and began firing. A bullet pierced through Jon-Jon's van, finding a home in Damian's shoulder. Another ripped through one of the children's throats that sat in Alexis's car. Yet another shattered the windshield of Julio's truck.

All heads turned to the roof to see Ben firing away at random. Ben fired again, hitting nothing but the night air before his gun clicked on empty chambers, dry firing at the survivors.

Gerty, weak and out of breath, stepped from her car and fired at him repeatedly, nearly collapsing from exhaustion in the process. One of her shots hit its mark. Ben fell backward, clutching at his gut. Gerty clutched at her chest, gasping for air. She wasn't certain, but thought she may have ripped her wound open. She pressed the pad to her chest, and fought to steady her haggard breaths.

The girl that had been shot in the throat came back after having only been dead for just under a minute. The others in the car had barely been able to get out with their belongings by the time she came to unlife.

Alexis rushed the other two children, Yussef and Stacey, to Jon-Jon's van. The three of them jumped in, leaving the dead girl in the car with it still running. Damian blocked out the pain as he helped the kids inside. It was a tight fit, but they would make it work.

Gerty got back in her SUV, taking a moment to catch her breath. Her breathing had become labored. And though the others noticed it, they kept it to themselves and chalked it up to her being out of shape and exhausted.

Assuming the worst, that Shorty was dead, Eddie led the convoy away from the school. The dead followed slowly behind, Shorty now among them. Ben lay on the roof of the school holding his gut. Through his fingers ran red rivers of blood. He knew his time was short, but he didn't care. He was looking forward to seeing what life was like on the other side. He was looking forward to tasting human flesh again.

13 TWO FOR THE ROAD

Eddie led the convoy through devastated suburban streets much like the ones he left behind, in a past life. A life that seemed as much a dream now as his dreams did then. They passed burned out cars, boarded up homes, and dozens upon dozens of dead people that staggered through the streets looking for something to devour.

They passed a large bus that sat upside down, half-in and half-out of the road. Smears of blood were visible on the inside of the few windows that remained intact. Every street was like the one before it. The blood left behind had stories to tell but no one had the time to read them. They were stories of struggle (that was for certain), whether they were tragic or triumphant no one would ever know.

To put his mind at ease, Eddie told himself that those boarded up homes had survivors inside. They were having apocalypse parties and sipping wine and eating fancy cheeses. Life was good beyond the boards, he thought. They were sheltered and secure, and playing Monopoly. They came across a few swarms that they needed to drive through to continue moving, so they did. But what damage it had done to their vehicles they wouldn't know.

Whether tired, delirious or both, Eddie swore he saw a ghost. As he continued driving the feeling came back repeatedly, even to the point where he thought he drove through one. No one else in the vehicle had mentioned anything, so he kept the thought to himself.

With no particular destination in mind they drove on, heading in the general direction of Titan City. Eddie stumbled upon a desolate road, free from housing developments. It looked like the start of an industrial complex but ended abruptly due to a train lying dormant on the tracks that cut the road in half. They turned around, heading back into the previous development in a quiet and dreadful little round trip. The people that comprised the convoy stared hopelessly out the window at a world they could no longer recognize.

Eddie heard the rapid sounds of automatic gunfire. He turned to see if anyone else could hear it. They did. They looked around for the source of the gunfire. But before they could find the source, the source found Gerty's SUV.

A military Humvee barreled into Gerty's SUV, caving in the entire side of the truck and sending it into a roll. The sounds of twisted metal and shattering glass broke through the noise of the night and would surely alert the dead to where they could find a fresh meal. The SUV landed on its topside as the convoy came to an abrupt stop, with many rushing out of their vehicles.

Inside the SUV Gerty wheezed her agonizing last breath. Many of her bones had been crushed on impact—it was a miracle she remained conscious at all. Corey, who was in the passenger seat, hung from his seatbelt with blood, and drool coming from his now mostly toothless mouth. His face was badly smashed, and he was surely bleeding internally. He couldn't move his arm, nor could he feel anything below his aching chest.

A woman from Corey's group, Lana, died on impact. She was in her late sixties, and ever since her husband passed years ago she wanted a peaceful death so she could be with him again. She never knew what happened. It was not peaceful, but at least it was quick. Next to her was another woman, one that had traveled with Gerty's group of survivors for a number of days. She had barely been more than a dead thing herself, having hardly muttered a word in the entire time she came to travel with these people. She never really did anything besides bite her nails and twitch nervously. No one remembered her name, if she ever gave it. She was awake, confused and terrified as the smell of gasoline burned her nose. No matter how hard she tried she couldn't get out of the vehicle. The door was so badly damaged it wouldn't move.

The Humvee remained upright. The driver lay slumped over the steering wheel. A man staggered out of the passenger side seat, holding his head, while another emerged from the rear of the driver-side rubbing his neck. Julio raced to Gerty's overturned wreck to help his friend Corey. Once he got a look at his condition, he pulled out his gun and walked over to the two soldiers.

"You mothafuckers!" Julio screamed, pointing the gun at the closest soldier.

"Easy, man," the one said. "It was just an accident," he proclaimed.

"Accident? I don't fucking care! You killed my friend," he screamed. His eyes were rimmed with hateful, angry tears that could've been venom.

Julio shot the soldier in the face, spattering blood on himself as well as the other soldier next to him. Eddie came behind Julio and snatched his gun quickly before he could fire again. The other soldier dropped to his knees crying. Those that gathered around never thought they'd see a soldier do such a thing. He took off his helmet, and his young face betrayed his uniform. He was only a kid.

"It was an accident. I'm so sorry. We were just fucking around, getting drunk. We haven't seen any other people in days," the kid soldier broke down into tears.

"Please, tell me you're ARMY," Eddie spoke.

"No. We found them at the recruiting office," he confessed. "It's where we stole the Humvee, and the guns. No one was there. We just took the shit."

Jon-Jon turned to look at the wreck. Through the mangled metal and shattered glass, he could see Gerty with a mouthful of flesh. They were all dead inside, yet they continued to move. No one was near the truck. He took aim at the gas tank and fired a shot. There was a small initial spark of an explosion, enough to set the wreck to fire. It burned bright and hot.

"Let's move," Jon-Jon suggested. "We'll be surrounded if we stay any longer."

"What about them?" Eddie asked.

"Leave'em," Jon-Jon said coldly.

"He deserves to die," said Julio.

"We didn't mean it," the boy cried.

His dead friend began to twitch back from the brink of death. Eddie filled the twitching creature's head full of bullets; the blood blew back on to him, and onto the crying boy who played soldier.

The driver of the Humvee began to stir. He lifted his head, blood spilling from his nose. Some of his teeth were missing, and his face was swollen. He looked out at the scene with blurred vision, not knowing what was happening. He pulled a gun from his side and took aim at Eddie—the only man he could see holding a weapon. He saw his friend dead, and his other friend on his knees crying. Anger moved his pains to the back of his mind. He shakily took aim and pulled the trigger. A three-round burst of fire cracked through the air.

Julio turned to the driver and charged at him with empty fists, but Jon-Jon's bullet beat him there. The driver slumped back, his hands clutching at his chest as blood gurgled up from the bottom of his throat. Dead things began to descend upon the area, though not many. And more would follow.

Damian was reluctant to leave the van. His wound continued to bleed but he wanted to be of help. Once he got out he could see that Julio was visibly shaken up. And when he could see the aftermath he knew why—he wished he had gotten out of the van sooner.

He ran to Julio's side, gun drawn. Though the driver was dead, Julio reached inside to pry the gun from his hands. It was an M162A Rifle, which was deceivingly light, though quite impressive to look at and hold. Julio felt an immediate surge of confidence. He turned to look at the crying mess of a drunken kid who stayed slumped down on his knees.

"Get up," Julio called to him.

Eddie turned to Julio. "What are you doing?" he asked quietly.

Julio ignored him. "Get up!" he yelled at the boy.

The boy refused to meet his gaze. "I don't want to die," he whimpered.

"Don't do this," Damian said, but remained at his side.

"I'm not doing anything. He is," Julio pointed at the boy who was now standing on rubbery legs. "Good, now take you're dead friend's gun over there," he told him.

The boy listened. He moved as slowly as the dead things that approached.

"Good, now shoot your friend in the face till he dies again," Julio ordered. He pointed at the driver of the Humvee whose dead hands tried to open the door.

The boy looked at him, his sorrowful eyes expressing a new emotion: disgust.

"Shoot him in the fucking face," Julio screamed.

The boy followed orders. He shot his friend repeatedly in the face, leaving nothing but a pile of red mush on top of his dead shoulders. Julio smiled, then raised his new weapon and shot the boy dead with a three round burst of gunfire. Several people screamed in opposition, but their protests couldn't stop the bullets.

"You're on your own," Eddie said. "You ain't coming with us," he said, holding his gun steadily in the direction of Julio's face.

"That's fine," Julio said, "I'm better off without you clowns. Been downhill ever since we met yall."

Julio looked at his friend Damian. He could tell he didn't approve of what just happened, but it was too late to take it back. He walked back to his truck. Damian looked at the faces of the new friends he made on the road, clearly sorry for his friends' actions. He shook Eddie's hand, and then Jon-Jon's and waived at the rest of them. He hopped in with Julio as the other people in his truck left, finding refuge with the others who would stay with the convoy.

"You know you're welcome to stick with us," Eddie called out.

Damian heard the words, but could only nod. He knew he was welcome to stay, but his loyalty was to his friend. Julio pulled the truck out of line and headed away as fast as his four wheels would take them.

The convoy drove off again, leaving nothing but regrets and the dead behind. The dead were too slow to follow. The dead boy who found it fun to play soldier rose from the tear-stained dirt and followed along with the other dead things.

14 TOMORROW NEVER KNOWS

West Virginia.
Mount Weather Special Facility.

In the deep recesses of The Mount Weather Special Facilities a woman by the name of Rachel Lucas, a biologist of some note, is examining the reanimated cadaver of a young soldier. She is dressed in a canary yellow HAZMAT suit with a clear visor and breathing apparatus. A similarly clad armed guard stands just outside of her room looking in through a large window.

There are thirteen other such rooms on the floor.

Rachel speaks into a recorder attached to her clothing. Her specimen is strapped down securely to an examining table with his arms and legs spread. The specimen's head is strapped down but it has full mobility of its jaw. Rachel has already taken blood, tissue, saliva, and all other possible samples from the specimen for examination later.

She circles the creature slowly, paying close attention to physical movements. She has orally noted, by way of her recorder, any and all observations, no matter how minor they may appear to be. There is also a video recorder set up in the corner of the room

She has worked for many days on her current specimen, seemingly without rest, but with very little to show for her efforts. Her superiors expect her,, to have an explanation for things that cannot be reasonably explained.

The specimen moans, his eyes follow her around the room. They are yellowed and dry, the blue color of his irises muted and nearly disappearing. The dead soldier moaned again, this time for a longer period of time. "Yyyrrrrrrrrgggggnnnuhhhh," is how it would be spelled if the sounds could be turned into letters.

She notes the verbalization and continues to spiral around the room. Her recorder beeps to let her know its memory is nearing capacity. The recorder appears to malfunction as it begins playback in reverse. Rachel hears a word she does not recall saying, and a big bright light bulb turns on in the back of her head.

She rushes out of the room to her computer, where she has downloaded all of her digital audio notes and can access her video recordings. Rachel begins to systematically review all of her notes in reverse playback, isolating the audio segments in which the specimen can be heard verbalizing. She has a small yellow paper pad next to her mouse and a black fine point pen. She writes down a number of words: pain, hungry, help, brains, flesh, meat, need, hell, hurts. Rachel, though not entirely convinced, believes that her dead specimen is communicating.

She listens to the segments repeatedly, and hears the words again. It's not her weary mind playing tricks. The words are there. Distorted? Yes, but there all the same. She's reminded of her youth when her and her older brother would spin their records in reverse in an attempt to hear satanic messages that never appeared. It would seem now the message had finally arrived.

She wants to share her findings with her colleagues and superiors, but knows that she has to have something more solid than a random series of words. Rachel suits up one more time to enter the examination room. She has a new recorder with a fully charged battery, and a number of questions to ask the dead soldier.

Rachel was never much for questions. She always preferred to find the answers for herself. Even in college when she was encouraged to ask questions she often hesitated, she'd much rather be the one to answer them.

This time was different though. Now she couldn't wait to ask her specimen a number of things. She only hoped he could understand her. She pulled a steel chair from the corner of the room and situated it in such a way that she could make eye contact with her specimen.

"Hello," she started, "can you understand me?"

The creature looked her in the eyes, moving its jaw in a biting motion. Rachel repeated her words exactly.

"Sssseyyy," the dead thing croaked.

Rachel played back her recorder and nearly jumped off her seat once she heard his response. She was slightly more disturbed now, more than she had ever been since the dawning of the dead things.

"What is your name?"

"Ssseellemmmmaaann," the soldier hissed.

"You don't remember your name?"

"Nnnnnn," it said.

"What do you want?"

"Hssselffffeeffiiillll."

Rachel had a sick feeling building up in her stomach. It soured her throat and made her heart beat rapidly.

"Why do you want life…and…flesh?" Rachel asked.

" Nnnniiiuurrrnniiappppppeessaee."

"What do you mean?"

"Yyyrrrrgggggnnuhhh," it rasped.

"If I feed you, will you answer my question?"

The dead soldier was silent for a moment, then garbled a sound, "Ssseey." It didn't sound like anything more than a primal grunt, more like a hissing, really. But once Rachel played it back she believed he said 'yes'.

Rachel shuddered and left the room again. She entered a larger room with additional specimens, limbs, and equipment. There were several guards, one for each specimen, and three lab technicians all in the same get up that Rachel wore.

She filled out a request for human tissue samples and handed the sheet to one of the technicians. He nodded and held out an extended hand in a gesture to a specimen that was strapped to an examination table. The specimen, an elderly female, had already been sampled. She had missing limbs, organs, skin, muscle tissue, you name it and it was sampled. She was a veritable buffet table of undead delicacies. Rachel pulled forth a small container and a scalpel and began to carve slices of her belly away.

She made sure to get a variety of selections and put them neatly into the container, all while the creature watched her with the one eye that hadn't been sampled yet. The specimen seemed almost sad, though Rachel had never witnessed any of them express emotion and realized she was projecting her own feelings instead.

Once Rachel had finished filling her container she placed the scalpel in a red HAZMAT container attached to the wall for later sterilization. She weighed the container and the previous technician noted it on her paperwork as she left the room.

Using a pair of surgical tongs, she dangled the strips of flesh over the specimen's mouth. The creature seemed uninterested in the rotting room-temperature meat that hung just near his lip. She tried the different selections of flesh, and still, the creature would not eat.

"You said if I fed you, you would answer my questions…why aren't you eating?" Rachel asked, as she began to question her own sanity. She was talking to a corpse, and trying to feed it. She wondered what she might do next—dinner by candle light?

"Gggniivvviiiilllll," it moaned.

Rachel played back the recording.

"No way," she said, "that is not happening, you can lie here and rot."

Rachel stormed out of the room, unsure of her own sanity.

15 UNEARTHED

It was nightfall at the Mourningside Cemetery and in its few mausolea the long dead twitched and writhed in their eternal resting places. They moved incredibly slowly, at first, but with each successive motion their decomposing remains miraculously gain a fluidity close to that of the other dead things walking the earth now. Similarly, the dead buried in the ground began to move in a way that would matter to those above. Their dead fingers created little tremors that began to splinter their coffins and move the dirt up and off. They were rising up from the bowels of the earth.

One woman, long dead and at the rear most mausoleum, staggered to her feet. She pushed the cement slab of her tomb to the ground, allowing herself to slither out and stand up on two feet again. It shattered into large chunks upon impact. She stood in the moonlit interment space on legs the color of rust. Her grey gown, which had been a white grown when she was laid to rest, bore the black beady fruits of mold.

In life she had the most beautiful blonde hair, but now she only had a few straw colored wisps that looked more like cobwebs than anything else. Her eyes had long ago withered away to dust. Her skin shriveled so tightly to her bones she stood as barely more than a skeleton in a burial gown. She took another step, landing uneasily as her weight shifted forward.

The dead woman had taken hours to move herself to the door of the mausoleum, and when she got there the door would not budge, it was secured with a chain.

Another long dead creature managed to push the cement slab off of its tomb to the ground, shattering it. The dead thing pulled itself out, falling to the ground, and the cracking of its bones filled the dark chamber. He was dressed in a fine black suit with a white shirt and a black tie. And all but the tie had been cut down the back. Though the two of them were family, this was the first time they were ever in the same room at the same time. One died before the other was ever born—more than a century apart, yet there they stood, meeting in death for the first time.

Dane watched the hodgepodge of a convoy slowly approach the roadblock at the southern side of New Haven. One vehicle took the lead, leaving the other vehicles a few car lengths behind. He radioed Sheriff Bruce Davis the moment he saw them approach—he was on his way.

Eddie pulled his vehicle to a stop. He was about four car lengths away from the roadblock. He opened the door and was about to step out—

"Do not move!" Dane ordered through his patrol car's PA system. "Stay where you are, and turn off your vehicle or you will be fired upon." Even he was surprised at how authoritative he sounded.

Eddie listened. He stayed where he was and turned off the vehicle, but kept his hand on his gun—just in case.?

The sheriff arrived with his truck and a few other officers and friends at his side. They stood at the roadblock, making their numbers visible to the convoy. Dane reached into his cruiser and turned on the roof and searchlights. He turned the searchlight to face the convoy. Dane then grabbed a handful of road flares and threw them toward the convoy, one on each side and one to the rear. He and the sheriff walked toward the lead vehicle with their weapons drawn: Dane held his service weapon, and Bruce held a shotgun with the dangerous end pointed at the lead vehicle.

"Driver, please step out of the vehicle with your hands up," Bruce ordered, as he approached the driver's side.

Eddie slid his gun over to his brother Joseph. Eddie's mother, Janice, put her hand on his shoulder as he slowly got out of the car. Eddie stood near the open door with his hands up. He was lit by the red glow of the road flares. He looked at the approaching men, trying to decide if they were good men or bad, and hoped they were at least reasonable despite which side of the moral coin they landed on.

Eddie couldn't help but remember the first time he was pulled over by a police officer. He was seventeen and had his license for barely a month. He was only going out to pick up a few things at the grocery store for his mother, and was on his way back when he was pulled over for not coming to a complete stop at a stop sign a few streets away from his home.

The police officer made him step out of the vehicle, insisting he had drugs on him. The police officer was sure of it, said he looked either drunk or stoned, and drove like it too. Ignorant of his rights, Eddie let the man search his mother's car. After an hour of searching and berating the young Eddie with the worst language and threats of violence, going so far as to jab his gun into Eddie's temple. The officer eventually let him go, and Eddie nervously drove home only to be followed the rest of the way.

Ever since then Eddie held a skeptical, yet somehow still respectful, eye to the authorities. It was a story he only told to his brother Joseph, who swore to never tell anyone—he didn't, of course. The two of them had always been tight like that.

"What is your intent," Davis asked, now mere feet away from Eddie.

"Just looking for someplace safe, sir," Eddie responded.

"Should've stayed home."

"Wish we could've."

"All these folks with you?" Davis asked, pointing to the convoy.

"Yes. We've been on the road for days. We were trying to get to Titan City…looking for our families."

"Well, lucky for all of you that you didn't make it there," Davis said. "Titan City is gone."

"What? What are you talking about?"

"Gone. The skyline is ash, kid. Bombs been dropping. LA is gone too."

"Fuck," Eddie said, his hands falling to his side, "you're serious?" he asked.

"Serious," Davis said. "So, I'll ask you this: what are your intentions now?"

"We just want someplace safe, sir. We won't last much longer on the road. It's been hell the last few days…we keep dying."

"We don't exactly have a Holiday Inn," Davis let down his guard, hanging his gun on his shoulder.

"We don't need much: a truck yard, a church, shit—a fence would be great. We got guns. We can be of help, there're thousands of those things out there--"

"Okay. Relax, I'll let you all in. But, you abide by my laws or you get the fuck out. We'll find you a place to stay, and those of you who can be of help will be put to use, understood?"

"Yes, sir," Eddie replied.

Sheriff Davis led the convoy into town. Eddie followed close behind him and Sal tagged along to make sure no one in the group veered off course. Davis pulled up to VFW hall, parked and got out. The hall was on a large plot of land and was fenced off. Davis instructed Eddie to lead the convoy into the fenced off area and gather everyone inside the hall.

The hall was a small brick building with a main entrance and a single back door. There were no windows on the building except the enclosure to the main entrance. There was a flag pole out front and on it hung a very clean and vibrant red, white, and blue flag. Just below that was a smaller Prisoners of War flag.

Inside the building were more flags, and plenty of framed pictures of the men and women who served their country valiantly. Though one wondered where they were now, when the world needed them.

A small bar area led the way to a larger open area for banquets, and behind that a kitchen. Davis sat on a metal folding chair, one of hundreds folded neatly against the wall. The building had power, one of the few that did, and as the room filled up people couldn't help but notice. Sal followed the last few people inside and ushered them into the rear of the hall.

"Welcome to New Haven," Davis said. Many in the crowd thanked him, some nodding in appreciation. "You are all welcome to stay here so long as you do what I ask of you. Don't worry, it won't be much. The first thing I need to know is if any of you have been bit or feel sick. If so, please step forward." No one did.

"All right, the second thing I need is for all of you to get some rest. You're no good to me, or anyone else, if you're exhausted. You'll be just another liability and if that's the case then get the fuck out." Davis paused, "I'll be back early tomorrow to see what it is that you guys can do to earn your keep while you stay in our lovely little community. If anyone has medical experience or can help in restoring power to the rest of the town I'll want to talk to you first. Till then sleep. If there's any food here help yourself. Good night." Davis stood up from the chair and walked through the crowd towards the door. He was thanked several times as he left.

Sheriff Davis and Sal left the building. Davis grabbed Sal by the arm gently.

"Keep an eye on them. Either you or someone else drive by every hour, make sure no one leaves the area," Davis told him.

Davis drove off in his truck, heading in the direction from which he came. He hoped he was doing the right thing. He hoped these people meant well, and were not looking to take advantage of others at such a horrible time for the human race. Sal sat in his cruiser for a few moments then, seeing that no one left the building, drove off too.

Everyone grouped off into different sections of the hall, looking for a place to rest and stretch out or just to talk. Scott headed toward the bar area and Judy followed behind along with Dawn. The two women found stools to sit on and Scott went behind the bar with the closest thing to a smile he'd had on his face in days. He rummaged around, tilting the bottles of various liquors, and wines towards the dim light to read the labels, though most he knew by the shape of the bottle alone. He found a bottle of Burgundy wine, popped the cork, and found three glasses and filled them up higher than any bartender he'd ever come across.

Scott was known by a few to drink wine as if it were fruit juice, often to his dismay. Scott was not a rich man, but business was always good. He wasn't much for bragging or showboating of any kind, if anything he was modest. He was born with a tongue made for drinking, and who was he to tell his tongue no.

Some of his friends grew snooty over the years, insisting on what wine should be drunk with what meal, and in what glass. Even to how it should be sipped. And it didn't stop with wine—it included bourbon, cars, clothing, and even home décor as well.

So, he would quietly rebel by pouring his wine in whatever glass he damn well pleased and gulping it instead of sipping it. He winced with every swallow. Judy and Dawn tried to follow by his example but after a gulp they returned to small sips. Regardless of whether sipping or gulping they were all in search of a little place called oblivion. How quickly etiquette had died.

Jon-Jon strolled over sometime after Scott had poured a second glass for himself and his bar-side companions. He was in search of a man named Walker and didn't care what color he was dressed him. He found him and began to empty his innards into a highball glass. Jon-Jon took a few hard swallows, then replenished the liquid and sipped.

Eddie sat with what remained of his family in the corner of the hall. His mother fell asleep almost as soon as she sat down. Joseph turned to Eddie, whose head rested on the brick wall behind him as his eyes stared up at the ceiling.

"What are we doing, Ed?" he asked his brother.

"I don't know…what do you want to do? If the city's really gone, then what's the point of going anywhere."

"I'm fine staying here. I don't want to die out there, and I don't want to lose you or ma." Joseph had a tremble rising in his voice.

Eddie didn't need to say, "I don't want to lose either of you too." But he did anyway.

"I wonder if anyone we knew made it out of the city. Maybe Uncle Bob? He was always a cool guy."

"Yeah, he was," Eddie agreed.

Joseph looked over to Alexis who was trying to put the children— Yussef, Stacey, Chris, Leela, and Nick—at ease so they would go to sleep. She looked back at him but then quickly turned her attention back to the kids.

Alexis had gotten used to Gerty taking charge of the kids. She had a gentle force about her that the kids responded to. Alexis didn't have that. She wouldn't be able to take care of these kids on her own. She knew others would help but not like Gerty did: Gerty made it her duty.

Alexis felt the pangs of guilt as she realized that she, herself, did not want it as a duty. To have the responsibility of another person's life in your hands was scary in its own right. Add to that a world where the dead were trying to eat you, and make it five lives as opposed to one. She was overwhelmed and Joseph could tell, but he didn't have the heart to help. His heart lay broken at home.

Old man Rickerbocker sat by himself biting his nails. He wanted to go out for a smoke but he didn't want to move, nor did he have any smokes left anyway. He also wanted to get up and join the others at the bar but he couldn't work up the energy to move, and he didn't want to wake up with a hangover, either. He wasn't even sure if he wanted to wake up. Each day seemed to be worse than the one before it, and he feared what tomorrow would bring. He just sat there. Unmoving. Hoping time would be so kind as to return the favor.

Frankie stood with a hand on Chung-Hee's shoulder and did his best to console him over the guilt he felt for Shorty's death. Chung-Hee had a feeling when he first met Ben that something evil was behind his somber eyes. He felt the exact opposite about Shorty. Shorty was a kind soul, an intimidating looking man but as gentle as the Jolly Green Giant. Chung-Hee couldn't help but feel responsible for his death—it was his plan after all. He hoped, in the back of his mind, that somehow he wasn't dead. That maybe he freed Ben and, unable to face the others, left on foot in an unseen direction. But despite what his mind hoped, his heart knew otherwise. And that was partly, if not entirely, Chung-Hee's cross to bear.

A group of four sat away from everyone else. They were all that was left of the group from the truck stop eatery. Among them were an older man with speckled and spotted skin named Angus, a chubby woman in her late thirties named Carrie, who only seemed capable of crying, and an Arabian man named Abdul-Ba'ith, who'd been accused multiple times of having something to do with the current situation—he's been fighting for his life from the living and the dead since the news broke, and a party loving, flip-flop wearing Floridian named Chuck who came to visit relatives—he barely survived the airport, and his tan was beginning to fade.

Chuck kept looking toward the bar area and after very little mental debate headed towards it. He too drank wine as if it were juice, in swallows not sips. After his belly warmed up from the wine he switched to whiskey. Chuck did love to party.

Morning came without incident in the hall. Sal had nothing negative to report on the newcomers when Bruce arrived. Bruce nodded with a smile and casually walked in. Sal's shift was over, so he headed home in hopes of sleep.

Bruce walked past the bar and, noticing the dirty glasses, and emptied bottles smiled to himself. He wasn't exactly happy about it, but understood. He hoped that they would in turn understand him. He walked to the spot where he addressed the group last night, and stood there patiently for a moment. The people who were awake watched him carefully, and those who still slept quickly awoke at the sound of his voice.

"Morning," Davis said loudly but not annoyingly so. And he deliberately left out the customary 'good'—he stopped saying 'good morning' the day the dead began to walk again.

"Morning," many replied.

"Time to earn your keep. Hope you got some rest 'cause you're going to need it." He paused to look at the crowd, knowing he had their attention he continued. "Any doctors, nurses, or emergency service workers among you?" he asked.

"Not exactly," Scott said, raising his hand slightly. "My wife and I are morticians—we can stitch. Also, we're both certified in CPR."

"Morticians? No shit, I'd think you two would be among the first to go," Davis said with a good-hearted smirk. "Well, that's good to know...let me write this down." He pulled out a small notepad and pencil from his breast pocket. "What're your names?"

"Scott."

"And, I'm Judy."

"Okay, great," Davis mumbled as he jotted down their names, putting the words 'stitches' and 'CPR' next to them.

"Law enforcement? Military?" Davis rattled off. No one stepped forward. "Okay. Has anyone ever worked for an electric company, or was at any point an electrician?"

"I was an electrician for most my life," Angus said as he stepped forward. "My arthritis is something fierce though...can't keep a steady hand anymore."

"Okay," Davis nodded. He jotted down the title 'electrician', while asking, "Name, sir?"

"Angus."

"Okay. Next up...construction?"

Frankie raised a hand, "I used to work part time for a few years."

"Me too," Chung-Hee added.

"I cut wood at Route 9 Lumber for two years," Jon-Jon said. He sounded unsure if it was relevant or not, and felt foolish either way.

"Okay, excellent. Names?" Davis asked as he jotted them down under 'construction'.

"All righty. My last question: any of you competent at using a firearm?" He was visibly surprised when nearly everyone raised a hand. "Perfect," he said with a big shit-eating grin. "I'm going to need a list of all your firearms...don't worry, I'm not looking to take them from you. I just want to know what you got and what kind of ammunition you're going to need. If you're not sure what you have, bring it to me and I'll find ammo for it. Every one of you that raised a hand will be pulling shifts at the roadblock, and throughout town. I'll see if I can get some walkie-talkies too."

Eddie spoke up. "We got a few already, Sheriff."

"A few more won't hurt, will it?" Davis said.

"No, sir, it won't."

"Angus, Frankie, Chung, and Jon, get your shit together and meet me outside in five minutes. We got a lot of work to do. The rest of you, rest up and take it easy on the booze. Either myself or someone else will be by in a few hours to start some of you off on guard duty or something." He began to mumble toward the end. "Maybe fixing up some breakfast for yourselves wouldn't be a bad idea, either. It's gonna be a long day."

Five minutes came and went. Jon-Jon and the group piled up in his van and followed Davis into town and toward the police station. Once inside, Davis offered them coffee, stale donuts, and cookies. None of them turned any of it down. They sat quietly among themselves while Davis gathered everyone at the station into one of the large meeting rooms. Davis rummaged through a supplies closet for the county map and a box of thumbtacks. He whistled and gestured toward the group as they shoveled crunchy cookies into their maws. As if they were caught doing something wrong they looked up and hurried over to him.

He briskly led them to the meeting room, where a handful of weary officers and tired trusted friends sat or stood around waiting. Davis tacked the map to a table and emptied the rest of the tacks on top of it. He instructed the newcomers to tack whatever places on the map they had come across that might be of interest. Red tacks were designated danger zones, green was designated for possible supplies, yellow were impassable roads, blue, which remained unused, was for other stationed survivors, and clear wasn't designated for anything but if they came up with another point of interest they'd have a color, or non-color as it were.

By the time they were done there were almost two dozen tacks on the map. Davis instructed everyone to update the map when any new info was available. Davis cracked his knuckles and decided it was time to let everyone in on his little plan.

"Since almost everyone is here I got an idea that can help to keep us all safe. It won't be easy, and we might end up hearing something from FEMA by then. But I ain't holding my breath. I want to wall off the town."

"And just how the fuck are we supposed to do that?" Keith asked with one eye opened wide and the other nearly pinched shut.

"Not really sure to be honest. I got a few ideas, but it'll take us a long time, and like I said, FEMA could make everything all right next week. But if they don't I want to be ready. First thing I want to do is get the power back up, after that maybe a town hall gathering with everybody in town to see what we can do about protecting ourselves," Davis replied, "which is probably something we should've done much sooner."

"Shit, man," Keith said. "Power sounds good, but we're already running on fumes. I know I'm exhausted--"

"Keith, that's why I want to wall off the town. We're all tired as shit. But if we put up some fences, get the power on and put up some security monitors then it'll be easier to get some shuteye. All I know is that if we keep doing what we're doing we won't make it on our own."

Jones spoke up. "Guys, let's just take this one step at a time, okay? Let's get the power back on. I'm getting real sick of pissing in the dark and hoping I don't make a mess. We can fight about the other shit after that."

They all agreed to take things one step at a time. Davis asked Jones and Keith to join him and the newcomers in heading over to the power and electric building in the hopes of returning power to the town. They obliged, and everyone headed out immediately. Jon-Jon grabbed another cup of coffee on the way out the door.

16 POWER TO THE PEOPLE

On the outskirts of town on a large barren plot of land sits the Power and Electric company building. Davis pulls up to the entrance gate of the fence, which he quickly finds to be locked. Their presence draws the attention of a dead thing that had wandered either to, or from, town. Its clothes were the color of sand, was torn and frayed, and was barely clinging to the wiry frame of the withered young man. His body looked like it had been run over several times: his head was crushed, its contents being contained by the leathery flesh which was stretched and ripped from head to toe. What remained of his hair stood up in frantic clumps. His arm was barely clinging to its shoulder, splinters of bone jutted from his forearms and mud like blood clung in gooey chunks around the wounds of his body. He was missing an eye, and it was uncertain if his other was there or if it was merely a wad of puss. He stumbled forward on swollen legs, and on shins as mangled as the branches of diseased trees.

Davis's stomach soured at its ghastly sight. He returned to his truck to retrieve his gun and a pair of bolt cutters. With the cutters slung across his shoulder he took aim at the shambling creature and fired. The creature slumped to the ground, reduced to a pile of twisted flesh. Davis walked over to it. Wincing from the stench he turned his head to the side and fired a second shot to the dead man's head. He returned to the fence, cut the lock and kicked the entrance gate open.

They drove in past the fence, pulling up toward the front of the building. The parking lot had a number of vehicles: employee vehicles, company vans, and repair trucks. Davis took note of this and headed toward the front doors with caution.

The rest of the group followed as Jones and Keith held the rear, both carrying shotguns. They found that the doors were locked. Their dark tint made seeing beyond them difficult. Not wanting to break the doors just yet, Davis led them around to the side looking for another way in. They came across another locked door then continued past it around the building in search of another. They came across a small loading dock and finally next to the dock, an unlocked door.

Davis slowly turned the knob and opened the door. A red light shone from inside the building as they entered. Standing in that dim red corridor they remained motionless, their breath slow and controlled, listening intently to the sounds of the building. Machines hummed and clicked. The place seemed empty.

Not knowing where to go, the group picked a direction and cautiously continued ahead. Davis led the charge as they passed a number of doors which turned out to be closets and offices, all of which were equally empty and seemingly void of any use. When the corridor turned, they headed up the side of the building and going toward the front.

At the opposite end of the hall, stumbling from around the corner was a man in dark blue work clothes. His tan boots were covered in blood and with each step he left some of it on the floor. Around his waist was a utility belt full of tools and blood. The creature cocked its head, and began moving its jaw. He looked as if he were trying to say something, but being that his throat was torn to shreds, he failed. Several more of the creatures came from behind the same corner. Their melancholy moans more than made up for the lack of vocalization from the first creature. They sounded hungry.

"I guess their shift just ended," Jon-Jon joked but didn't laugh.

"Let's go back the other way," Davis suggested.

The group went back in the direction of the dock only to be halted again. Coming from the far end of the corridor was another group of equally disgruntled and vocal employees. With few options they turned around again, heading to the first group of undead attackers. They tried the doors within the gap between them and the dead: a set of restrooms, followed by a locker room, and a closet after that. They were now mere feet from the first set of attackers when the others rounded the corner behind them.

Frankie and Jones readied their weapons. Angus looked ready to have a heart attack and make a trade to the opposing team. Keith pulled a flask from his back pocket and tipped his head back, letting the warm wet whiskey burn his belly. Davis tried the last door, it opened and he rushed inside. The others followed. Jon-Jon took aim at the first dead man they had come across and fired. The bullet grazed the thing's face and ricocheted off the wall at the end of the corridor. He kept his handgun pointed at the fearless foe. He stared at him, wondering what the fuck the point of it all was. Wondering if he too would walk around like that, if he'd even know, or care, deciding that none of it mattered he fired again. The dead man died again, dropping to the ground. The maggots in his throat held steady, oblivious to the fall of man.

Frankie pulled Jon-Jon by the arm and Davis flung the door shut behind them, giving Jon-Jon a look that would've shaken him a few weeks ago. But not today, and probably never again.

The room they stood in was a small cafeteria. If they had an appetite then they would've had plenty to eat. But being that they wanted to get away from the things clawing at the other side of the door they decided to head to the other door in the room.

That door led to a small kitchen with vending machines, which emptied into the building's central corridor. They frantically moved into the corridor. Davis looked straight ahead while the others spun around nervously. The front doors were at their backs. One door led to another, and somehow they ended up in front of a door with big bold letters stating CONTROL ROOM. Davis turned the handle of the door, pushing forward. It opened only a few inches before it was stopped by something on the inside. Davis pushed harder, and then rammed his shoulder into the door, but it didn't budge. The sounds and smells of the dead traveled through the air. They were coming. Davis attempted to ram the door again when they heard a voice from behind the door.

"You dumb zombies keep trying to get in here when you know it ain't gonna happen," screamed a man from behind the door as he violently stabbed a thin pipe through the space between the door and its jamb.

"We're not zombies!" Davis screamed back. "Let us the fuck in!"

There was a brief moment of silence and some shuffling from

behind the door. It opened further and a scruffy, squinty-eyed fellow peeked past the door. His eyes grew as wide as a pair of full moons at midnight and his brow furrowed when he realized that they in fact weren't zombies. He stumbled backward and pulled the door with him as Davis and the others charged in. The man scratched at his wild beard with grimy fingers, clearly speechless.

He eventually found a few. "You sure ain't zombies," he muttered. His eyes grew wide once again. "Are you cannibals?"

Frankie was flabbergasted. "Are you fucking crazy, man, seriously? You think we want to eat you?"

"Never know. That's what they always end up doing in the movies." He trailed off as he stared into the sea of faces that stared back at him.

"This ain't the movies, and this isn't some voodoo bullshit!" Frankie barked. "Those dead things are gonna be trying to get in here any minute...is there another way out of here?"

"Slow down, Frank," Davis said. "We're not leaving till we can turn the power back on." He turned toward the odd bird whose nest they had disturbed. "You must work here. Can you put the town's power back on...uh, what's your name?"

The old man laughed. "Oh! Sure! Let me push my magic button then we can all trot on out of here on the yellow brick road too, while we're at it."

"You don't have to be an asshole," hollered Angus.

"Easy Grandpa," the man yelled back. "I've been in here a long time with nothing but the company of the dead and a stomach full of vending machine garbage. I've also been sleeping against the door for the however the fuck long I've been in here. And now you clowns think I can just wave a magic wand and make all the lights in town work?"

"Okay, can we all just calm down for a minute," Jon-Jon chimed in. "Sir, my name is Jon, most people call me Jon-Jon. What's yours?"

"Topher," the man said after a long pause.

"It's good to meet you, Topher. Now, would you be willing to help us get the power up and get the hell out of here?" Jon-Jon asked.

Topher had a sour look on his face but nodded. "Sure thing. But before I can be of any help I need to know why the power is out. Something had to cause it and we need to find out what."

The others looked at each other as if this was the first time they considered that something specific (more specific than dead people getting up and attacking the living) had to cause the power outage.

"Like what?" Davis asked.

"Could be anything. Maybe a downed line, or a squirrel could've gotten into a transformer and shorted it out. A car accident, fire, you get the idea."

"Any suggestions on how we can find that out?" Angus stepped in.

"I got a few."

"Guess that means we need to get the hell out of here," Jon-Jon said.

"Guess so," Topher replied.

"Unless those things find something else to chase after, we're going to have to fight our way out," Davis said.

"Not necessarily." Topher paused once he realized he had everyone's attention. "So long as we're as quiet as can be, sometimes the noises the machines make get their attention."

"Then what, they just leave us alone?" Angus asked.

"Yep. For a little bit. They always come back, though—it's like they know I'm in here." Topher said.

They sat quietly for a good long time. Longer than any one of them could bare. Jon-Jon was ready to open the door and take his chances fighting them off, as was Davis and Frankie. Angus was as calm as a cucumber. Topher looked like he wanted to talk, but obviously couldn't. Keith looked around the room, hoping to find some sort of alcohol, but knew there wouldn't be any. And Jones began to tap his fingers, perhaps the most restless of them all, though in no hurry to lead the charge out of the room.

More time had passed, and the restlessness reached a boil. The dead things just outside the door did not relent for a moment. The noises inside the building were not enough to throw them off. Topher admitted that that it had never happened before. And he assumed it had something to do with how many people were in the room now, as opposed to just himself.

There was no other way out. No vent to crawl out or a window to squeeze through. There was only the door they had come in through—one way in, one way out. Keith, Jones, and Frankie stood ready with their shotguns. Davis directed them to stand to the side of the door, keeping as much distance from each other as possible. He had Frankie stand behind the others, as a back-up shooter, and Keith knelt down on one knee—he'd hit them low, while Jones hit them high.

Jon-Jon stood near Frankie, shaking with adrenaline and fear. His palms were sweaty and he moved his handgun from one hand to the other. Davis had lent Angus a service weapon and he clutched it clumsily while aiming it at the floor. His hands were shaking badly from the arthritis, and beads of sweat rolled down the side of his face.

Topher gripped his pipe and shuffled around in a semicircle. Davis held onto the doorknob with his left hand, his handgun in his right. He pulled the door open and backed away in one fluid motion, bringing the handgun into the firing position immediately.

The dead things practically fell into the room, having been pressed against the door. And the ones in front were pushed forward by the numbers behind them. Keith fired when Davis was out of the way and nearly cut the first few in half. The noise exploded in the room, putting cotton in everyone's ears. Jones took off one of the creature's heads, sending gray matter spattering along the door jamb and walls.

As the first few dead things fell to the ground, others staggered forward. They were clumsy and stumbling over the bodies of their fallen brethren but were still faster than they had any right to be. Keith pumped his weapon and fired away, blowing out the leg of the next deader, obliterating its knee entirely. Davis took a kneeling position as well, and began to take well-aimed shots at the creatures' heads. One more deader dropped, then another, forming a small pile at the foot of the door. The others stood behind the three men on the frontlines in amazement. They were ready for action, but glad that the others were making headway.

There were still a good number of deaders just outside the door: too close to move outside, but too far to make any more surefire shots. Davis readjusted his position to the other side of the door, nervously footing around the dead limbs strewn about the doorway. He stepped on a dead hand, crunching the fingers, and immediately jumped off. It was the only time anyone had seen him even remotely nervous.

The dead things outside lurched closer to the door. Davis raised his weapon and fired several shots, emptying his weapon. He stepped back, ejecting the cartridge from his handgun and pulling another from his belt. Keith stumbled up off of his knee and stepped toward the pile of bodies. He stepped uneasily on top of them, making his way out of the room. His foot slipped in the gore and he fumbled forward loosing his grip on his weapon; they both fell forward out the doorway.

The others in the room gasped and raced forward. Jones in the lead ran over top of the bodies, nearly stumbling himself. He raised his weapon toward the nearest fiend and fired, taking off most of its shoulder and bits of its neck. The creature continued to move forward, unmoved by the force of the shot. Davis was right behind him, and took aim at the dead thing's head. He fired twice and the creature slumped to the ground like a heavy sack of laundry. Keith stumbled to his feet, half covered in gore and looking frantically for his weapon. Jones took aim at another dead thing as the others tiptoed out of the room over the bodies of the fallen dead.

Angus tripped over a dead man's hand and Topher tried to grab him but was of no help. Angus fell backward toward one of the dead creatures. Jon-Jon fired at the creature and it went down but kept moving. Angus fought hard to get up but he was old and couldn't move very quickly. The dead thing grabbed Angus' arm as he tried to push himself upward. He pulled but the dead man's grip was firm. Due to the angle, no one could get a clear shot at the creature. Angus raised his own weapon and fired at the creature's head, but the gun didn't fire. "Shit!" Angus thought. The dead thing pulled itself close enough to bite and took a chunk out of Angus' arm. He screamed a high-pitched shriek as the dead things crooked, yellowed teeth tore a chunk of his skin out. Davis rushed over to him, shooting the creature in the face repeatedly, the dead man's face splattered all over Angus's face and the floor.

Davis helped pull Angus to his feet. He was as white as a ghost, and with good reason. He clutched at his arm and handed Davis the gun he had lent him.

"Here's your fucking gun," he said grimly.

Davis took the weapon and looked it over quickly. "You left the safety on," he said defeated, upset knowing the man was as good as dead.

"Figures," Angus replied bitterly.

Keith and Jones made quick work of the last few deaders. The small area was thick with gun smoke, cordite and rot. It followed them as they made their way back out of the building. Once they reached the loading dock Topher began searching through the receiving desk. After a brief moment he found a ring of keys and held them up triumphantly.

"What's that?" Davis asked.

"Keys to one of the repair trucks, I hope."

Davis nodded. With all the gunplay he'd nearly forgotten what he had set out to do. He had only wanted to get out of the building and stop the ringing in his ears.

Frankie led them out of the building. He was startled by the darkening evening sky and cool breeze. They'd been in that room most of the day, leaving them tired, hungry, and feeling like they had just been robbed.

Topher tried the keys in several of the repair trucks before one of them roared to life. He laughed with excitement and slapped the steering wheel hard. Davis smiled.

***

They followed Topher around the outskirts of town, looking for what could be the cause of the power outage. They drove slowly down the desolate streets. It was getting dark and they didn't want to pass by whatever it was that was preventing New Haven from having electricity. As they drove past a deer carcass lying by the side of the road Topher expected it to get back up and try to eat him. Fortunately it didn't.

By luck, or the grace of God they came across a telephone pole. It leaned slightly toward the opposite side of the road on a splintered base. Half in the road and wrapped around the base of the pole was a midsize sedan. Its windshield looked like a massive glass spider web. Tiny bits of cubed glass sprinkled the hood and pavement. Inside the sedan something moved.

Topher pulled close to the pole, looking for a downed wire but saw none. The impact could have knocked it loose or blown a fuse in the power line. The only way he could be certain was to go to the top and find out. The pole looked like it would stay up long enough for him to check. If they ever got around to it, and wanted to keep the power on, it would need to be repaired. Topher nervously got out of the truck with Davis and the others close behind him. They slowly approached the car.

Standing at the driver's side door of the sedan, Bruce Davis looked in. It was a sorry sight for sure but Davis just looked at the dead thing in disgust.

"Look at this thing," he said, almost to himself.

"How long has he been like that," Jon-Jon asked.

"Power's been out for days, Five, I think..." Davis said. "But that's not the sad part. Here this thing is, this dead fucker, and he can't get himself out of his seatbelt. And yet he and his kind are killing off the world as we know it."

"Doesn't make any damn sense," Jones said from behind Davis.

"No, it don't," Angus said, still clutching his throbbing arm.

The creature writhed in its seat, the seatbelt held him firmly in place. The blood-caked steering wheel was close to his chest, probably the reason the man died. His legs looked cramped, his face swollen and his teeth lay scattered on top of his body and seat. Thick syrupy blood decorated the interior. The thing's hands reached crookedly out of the window, grasping at the air in hopes of snagging a morsel of flesh from Davis or one of the others. Davis raised his weapon and fired, illuminating the night with gunfire.

"We'd better move quickly," Jones said. "If there're any more of these things around they'll have heard the shot and come looking for dinner." He was eager to be done.

"I'll need one of you to operate the crane for me so I can get to the top and have a look at the transformer," Topher said.

"Sign me up," Frankie volunteered.

Topher showed him everything he needed to do and was slowly, but surely, making his ascent. He double-checked his tool belt, making sure he hadn't left anything in the truck. He hadn't. He shone his flashlight to the top of the pole. Most of the daylight had disappeared and they were left with the blue-ish-purple haze of early evening. The light illuminated the pole-mounted transformer—from Topher's vantage point it seemed fine. As he reached the top however he could see burn marks on the transformer.

Once he opened the unit, he noticed the circuit breaker had opened. He was surprised a fuse hadn't blown, but was relieved that the job would be even easier than he had anticipated. He simply closed the circuit breaker allowing the electricity to be distributed again. He monitored it momentarily, making sure it didn't open again and when it didn't he closed the unit and signaled Frankie down below to bring the crane back down.

On his descent he shone his flashlight around. He looked at the surrounding area and noticed nothing beside the streetlights flickering back to life.

"Looks like you did it," Jon-Jon called up to him.

"Easy as pie," he replied, and after saying it realized how hungry he was. "Now, how about getting me some food, huh? And maybe a toothbrush? Then we can go around some more and see if there's any other downed lines."

"You got it. A bar of soap wouldn't kill you either," Davis smiled, looking at the lights from town.

Angus' skin grew pale in the darkening evening. His arm burned and he couldn't bring himself to look at the wound. He knew what it meant, people died quicker from a bite—he didn't know why, no one did. What he did know, or thought he knew, was that it wasn't the bite that turned you into one of the dead things. No matter who died and how, they came back—bite or no bite. Some took longer than others, and the bitten could last a day or more before dying and returning. He'd seen it happen too many times over too few of days. He didn't want to wait for it to overtake him. He wanted to die on his own terms—it was all he had left, and he was lucky to have that much.

"I used to have a drug problem," Angus said.

"What's that?" Keith said, having had one as well.

"I started out smoking marijuana—everyone was doing it—till they started cracking down on it. Then I was doing coke, though that was harder to get and eventually I got hooked on heroin—thank you very much Miss Morphine." Angus looked at the stars. "Once I got home from 'Nam I was hooked. It took a good woman, my wife Betty, to get me unhooked. But I was never really unhooked, I'd think about it at least once a day, not all day mind you, but in passing—quickly, you know."

"Okay," Frankie said, taken back by how much Angus was sharing with them and at such a time.

"Sorry to ramble...I guess what I'm trying to say is that...I want…I want you to…to kill me. I want one of you to ram as much heroin into my veins as it takes to kill me," he stared at Davis.

"Are you serious?" Davis asked.

"Yes, sir, I can feel myself dying. I can feel this little darkness beating in my heart, gnawing at my mind. I can feel it in my gut, like I felt back in Cambodia, only this time there is no hope." Angus began to cry. "Please, give a dying man a blindfold and one last smoke," he pleaded. "Death has her cold fingers wrapped around my throat."

"If that's what you want," Davis said, holding back tears for a man he'd only know in the last few hours. A man by all accounts he should care less for. Regardless he empathized with the man, and hoped to hell he would never be in his place. If death is what he wanted, then death is what he'd get.

17 ONE MORE TIME TO KILL THE PAIN

Under the grassy surface of Mourningside Cemetery the long dead clawed their way upward. Some of them moved slower than others, but some, very few, moved faster. Moving through the dirt was no easy task, hundreds of pounds of dirt lie on top of each dead individual. But they didn't have to worry about pain or breathing. Without the woes of the living to keep them down they continued their deliberate rise toward the surface.

Below the heavy grey block of concrete we all get when we reach the end of our lives clawed the hand of the man whose name was etched in stone, to forever remain at peace under the ground. It would seem he was not at peace, however, as something stirred him back to life. He clawed and fingered his way through the dirt pulling himself upward. His mouth and throat filled with dirt. His fingertips would have started bleeding days ago had he any blood left in his body. The make-up that sat heavy on his face during his viewing rubbed off long ago. He was persistent, as were all the dead underground, the long dead, and he won the unannounced race to the top.

The ground swelled and pulsed as his fingers flicked through the damp blades of grass that lie over him. A moment later his entire hand and part of his wrist burst through the ground and grasped at the air, as if choking some invisible throat. Eventually he pulled his entire body from the blanket of dirt. What skin could be seen through the sheen of dirt and rot was as pale as the maggots and worms that clung to his rotting corpse. He was buried, as most men, in a simple suit slit down the back. His shoes and socks didn't make it to the top, not that he cared. As his body slumped to the ground some of the dirt knocked off. His gaping maw full of dirt emptied to the ground as well, though much of it was left dangling from the top of his mouth and stuck at the back of his throat. Other hands began to find their way to the surface as well.

***

Behind the cemetery, in the shadow of the woods sitting on top of a large rock were best friends Brian and Chris (whom everyone called Teets). They were almost old enough to drive, though they both knew how to already. They snuck away most nights in one of their parents' cars to find a place to smoke up. They dared not do it too close to home. Getting busted would surely be a buzz kill, and neither wanted that. As high as the sky would allow was their preference and Mary Jane was their pilot. The ship of choice for the evening was a dutchie.

Teets unwrapped the vanilla flavored Dutchmaster cigar and began to lick the entire thing. Getting it wet enough so it wouldn't crack. Then he bit off the end of it and spat it out. Then he carefully picked at the outer leaf and unrolled gently, hoping it was wet enough to come off in good shape. Then he removed the cancer papers and gutted the tobacco.

Teets sat cross-legged at the top of the rock. He had an issue of Batman that was bagged and boarded in his lap. Inside the comic he had rolling papers and a razor, in case he needed them: they were always there and his parents would never think to look in a comic book for such things. He emptied the bag of sticky-sweet-smelling buds onto the board and broke it apart, digging out the seeds and stems. He liked to chew on the stems as he rolled, so when he found them he popped them into his mouth.

Brian was watching Teets work his magic. Brian preferred the ease of a bowl or the soothing sounds of a bong but there was something about a dutchie that he just couldn't resist. Rolling wasn't his strong suit, so he studied Teets' technique. He could roll a good joint, wasn't too bad with a blunt, but when it came to a dutchie he just couldn't pull it off.

With the world being the way it was they had been rationing what little they had left of the Lady Jane. Be it boredom, or a loss of appetite the two couldn't wait to get out and partake in the old ritual. Most of the time they would smoke in the back room of the gas station where they worked at the edge of town, but it had been closed for a few weeks now.

Teets rolled the unwrapped blunt around the hefty helping of buds, smoothing it out as he did so. He wrapped it tight, but not too tight, then licked it around a few times and ran the lighter around it to dry it up. Teets dusted off his comic and tossed it to Brian who threw it in his backpack. The work was done, and now it was time to set the lady on fire and watch her burn. Mary Jane, how the boys love you!

Laying on the giant rock with their eyes to the sky, the two youngsters passed the dutchie back and forth: puff, puff, give. As the orange tip of burning bud and browned leaf continued to slowly disappear the two grew increasingly stoned. Stoned stupid was what they were, giggling like it was their second or third time, which was years ago. They both swore neither got high their first time, but they did, which is why there was a second and a third and so on.

Unsure if they could even finish, they began to hear noises—paranoia was beginning to set in. Every rustling of the leaves was an FBI agent. They've been watching them for years. They finished Mary off, pinching their fingers together in a desperate attempt at one more hit. Brian, trying to get one last kiss from the lady, burnt his finger and dropped the tail end of the blunt into the leafy bottom of the woods. Teets slapped his arm.

"Fucker, there was another hit left in that."

"Dude, it was kicked." Replied Brian with a dry tongue.

"Whatever...let's get something to drink. I got some Dr. Pepper at my place."

"Awesome."

They slid down the rock with backpacks in hand. Their eyes were red and their mouths dry. They tried to play it cool, but they were too damn high to do so. They giggled all the way back to the hole in the fence at the back of the cemetery. Once they got there, they froze in mid step.

"Dude, are you fucking seeing this?" Brian asked.

"I don't want to be, Bri," Teets mumbled.

"It's like Night of the Living Dead out there."

"No, way, it's more like Return of the Living Dead." Teets replied.

"Fucking zombies, man, that shit ain't right," Brian said as his mouth got dryer. "We need to tell everybody—I can't believe they're coming out of the ground!"

"Yeah, I guess whatever's been happening isn't terrorists, or rabies—well, I guess it still could be--"

"Shhh," Brian cut him off. "Do you hear that?"

"Hear what?"

From behind them staggered one of the long dead that must have found its way through the hole in the fence. Most of its clothing was now gone and its skin looked like dirt covered bark. The thing looked more like a mummy than any living dead thing the two of them had ever seen in the movies. It didn't have any eyes, just holes filled with dirt. It raised its hands to grasp at the back of Teets' neck but Brian pulled him forward and began to run.

"Fuck, come on man, RUN!"

"Shit, shit, shit! Stoner's always die in the movies, dude," Teets cried.

"This ain't the damn movies, just run," Brian hollered as his baggy jeans almost tripped him up.

They ran like hell was hot on their heels. The dead thing followed, slowly, very slowly.

18 SITUATION DEGENERATES

Sal was running on two hours of very unfulfilling sleep. He drank coffee after coffee as he fought to keep his eyes open. Now he was riding around town on patrol, looking for any signs of dead invaders. He hadn't found any and hoped that meant there weren't any to be found. He blinked so often and at such lengths it was possible that he drove past one and hadn't noticed.

So, when Brian and Teets came running up to the car he was surprised because they appeared to come out of nowhere. His eyes were probably shut for a good minute and only opened at the noise of their hands slapping on the window, which caused his heart to do a cartwheel. Sal braked, and threw the car in park. He looked pissed off, not at the two of them but at being awake when he really didn't want to be.

He stepped out of the car and made a shut-the-fuck-up kind of motion with his hands and face as Brian and Teets rambled incoherently.

"What the fuck are you two idiots saying?"

"Dead people at the cemetery…" Teets said, out of breath and breathing hard.

"That's usually where dead people go—hey, you fuckers been smoking up? You reek to all hell! God damnit!"

"No, just a cigar--"

Sal cut Brian off mid-sentence. "Can it, don't really give a shit right now. You kids ain't doing any coke or speed, are you?" Sal asked, wanting it for himself.

"No sir, definitely not!" Brian began to worry.

"Uh-uh," Teets said as he shook his head.

"Hmm, all right. Now, what the hell is going on? Spit it out!" Sal barked.

"Dead people at the cemetery...are coming up out of the ground," Teets told him.

"No shit?"

"No shit," they both replied.

"Get in the back," Sal said, opening the door.

Brian and Teets looked at each other. They were stoned stupid, reeking of weed and carrying some, along with rolling papers and blunts and getting into the back of a police car. After a moment of hesitation they got in. Once inside their high began to come down.

Sal drove up to Mourningside Cemetery and could see from inside the car that a number of things had dug their way to the surface, and still more were in the process. He couldn't believe it. They had searched the area days ago, and had kept an eye on it in passing while patrolling the town. Now, there were dozens of dead people walking around after digging themselves up and out of their eternal resting plots.

It was just like in the movies, dirt covered hands reaching up from out of the ground. Insanity! Sal thought, but they were all seeing it. This was not sitting well with Sal. This had to be something more than a virus, or a disease, he thought. It had to be God...or the Devil. It had to mean the beginning of the end. It had to, he thought.

Sal stepped out of the car and walked over to the tall iron gates that served as the entrance to the cemetery. After their initial search of the grounds weeks ago the police had locked the gate with a chain, which still held. The dead things clawed at it and as Sal approached the gate, they reached for him too, their skin ripping as they did so. He stood staring at them for a moment, half expecting to see his parents, both of which were buried there, and was slightly relieved when he didn't. He unclipped his walkie-talkie.

"Sheriff, we got ourselves a little situation," Sal said.

Sal stood waiting for a reply as he stared past the gate looking for his parents and praying he wouldn't find them, praying that they were at peace and didn't want to rise up against the living. Sal wasn't much for praying, usually only when something bad had the possibility of happening. Faith has a way of showing up when people need it, and it has a way of disappearing when they don't.

"Kinda busy…what's up," Davis responded.

"Dead people at the cemetery," Sal mumbled.

"That's where they should be."

"Yeah, well, they're coming up from the fucking ground."

"Fuck."

"Yep."

***

Davis handed Angus the needle. His belt was wrapped tight around his wrinkled old arm, the tail of it pulled taught from his mouth. His arthritic hand quenched in a fist while the other shakily took the needle from Davis. They sat on the tail of Davis' truck under a streetlight near the edge of town. Angus pushed the needle into his vein and pressed its contents into his blood. He opened his mouth and the belt around his arm loosened. His head tilted back and he moaned a sigh of pleasure. Davis moved away as Angus began to spasm. His breathing became labored and he went into shock. He fell off the truck and spasmed on the ground. Davis drew his handgun and fired into the man's head. He waited, and moments later as Angus began moving again Davis fired again, and again, and again.

19 MOTHS TO THE FLAME

When Davis showed up at Mourningside Cemetery Sal had managed to contain the long dead within the cemetery yards. With the help of the two stoners, he went around the outside of the grounds and found a few holes in the fence. The concrete walls, though, looked fine. He kept rope in the trunk of his cruiser, and used it to tie together the severed ends of the fence as best he could. It would help for a little while, but the dead things would eventually tear through it—he'd deal with that when the time came.

Through their trek around the grounds they came across the dead thing that had startled the two stoners earlier. This time the deader was accompanied by two companions who looked no better for wear. Sal had emptied a full clip into their heads, but they continued to stumble forward with chunks of head and face missing. He reloaded and attempted to shoot them some more.

"It's not working, man," Brian began to shout.

Sal snapped back at him. "No shit, kid."

"Fuck, oh, fuck, what're we gonna do now," Teets added.

"Shut the fuck up," Sal yelled, emptying the rest of his clip into the dead trio's heads.

"We got to burn 'em up," Sal said, almost to himself.

Davis came with the only two flame-throwers he had in the armory. They had rarely been used, not in the time since Davis had been a part of the department. They were old, but functioning, and functioning well enough to burn up the dead. He handed one to Sal and then strapped the large bulky unit to his own back. Sal began to fasten his on as well. Davis stepped toward the cemetery gates igniting his flame-thrower. He throttled the trigger, and the flame went from small enough to burn a finger to large enough to burn off your face.

At the gates, Davis throttled the flame all the way to burn-off-your-face levels and ran it from left to right setting fire to the dead things that reached through the gate. They did not flinch, or pull back from the fire. They didn't even moan in protest. They moved forward, reaching through the gates to grasp at them. There arms becoming black and smoldering like trees after a forest fire. There was little left to burn but weathered skin wrapped around bone.

The recently deceased creatures were much easier to burn. Their flesh took almost as quickly as their clothes did, but not these. These almost refused to burn. Davis didn't sweat it though, he kept at it, and eventually they fell to the ground smoldering. Given enough time, just about anything will burn.

By the time Sal had joined him near the front of the gate the two stoners had taken off. They began jogging away toward home, their highs long gone. Sal stood a few feet from Davis and followed his lead. The two of them knew that the flame-throwers wouldn't be enough for all the dead things inside the cemetery, so they stood at the gate and let them come to the fire. Like big dumb bugs buzzing into a zapper they silently staggered toward the fire.

Maybe the fire was their salvation, Sal wondered, a way for them to move on? Why else would they walk right into it without the slightest hesitation? Were they just that dumb? Or, did they know it could kill them? Sal shook his head, trying to shake himself from his thoughts and focus on the task at hand. He was tired and his mind needed sleep to work out his thoughts. He wondered if he'd ever sleep again.

Before too long, the tanks to the flame-throwers ran dry. The gates were swarmed with the well-dressed, long dead. Those that burned had melted to the iron gates and then slumped into the dirt and gravel, unmoving. Whatever it was inside of them that made them tick was burned to a crisp. The others would have to wait their turn.

Davis wondered why the dead and buried—the long dead—wouldn't go down with a bullet to the head. It worked for the fresher ones, why not for them as well? He couldn't shake the overbearing feeling of dread that began to blanket him as his thoughts wandered. Few things ever got under Davis' skin, and nothing had gotten under it like this. In Davis' world you lived and then you died, then you rotted away in the ground. There was no heaven and no hell, and there certainly was no resurrection.

The flame-throwers had overheated. The tanks themselves were cool but the nozzles were steaming hot and Davis nearly burned his hand trying to take the bulky unit off his back. He eventually managed to, but only after singeing the hair off his arm with the nozzle. Sal squirmed out of his just fine, and the two of them placed their overheated packs on the back of Davis' truck.

"I'm getting sick of smelling burnt skin, man," Sal said.

"Me too. Can't get it out of my nose, but what's the alternative?"

"None, I guess." Sal scratched at his neck.

Davis pointed at the cemetery. "What'ya think we should do about this?"

"Shit, only thing we can do is to keep burning them. But those flame-throwers aren't gonna cut it. They're good, don't get me wrong, but maybe we should just douse the place in kerosene—toss a few buckets over the walls."

"Yeah, these things are neat and all, but my back's already killing me from it—fuckers way a ton. I just can't believe this shit…no more surprises, please."

Sal patted him on the shoulder. "You said it brother. Wanna drop these off and get the kerosene?"

"No, no I don't, but what choice do we have?" Davis walked to the driver's side.

The truck drove off leaving the long dead to cool off. More limbs ripped through the earth to pull up their bodies. There was only a few more deaders still underground, soon all whom were buried there would be above ground. Except for one small rotted baby too tiny to sift through the earth.

20 STANDING STILL

With the majority of power back on, and the long dead being put back to rest at Mourningside Cemetery, Davis moved on to the next step in his plan; a town meeting. He had everyone who wasn't working on either one of the roadblocks or up at Mourningside, go house to house to inform every one who stayed in town to assemble at the town hall at sundown.

By the time sundown came around the job was barely finished. Everyone who was capable came to the meeting. Jeff and Walter Caulfield came out while the rest of their family stayed home. They both agreed that the children had no reason to come out to the gathering and their better halves were content to stay the course.

People were excited to be outside, and some of them took it as a sign that things were on there way back to normal. Though that certainly wasn't the case. Jeff and Walter stood at the back of the room, nodding and smiling at everyone. The air was full of small talk and speculation.

Once everyone was gathered Davis began the meeting. It took him a moment or so to quiet the room down, but he eventually did. He asked how everyone was doing and if they were in dire need of anything. He asked if anyone had come across the dead, and most had. Some had dispatched creatures while others avoided them altogether. Walter asked about the city bombings, and if they should be concerned about nuclear fallout. Davis went at length about being better safe than sorry. He used it to touch on other subjects as well but didn't think fallout would be much of a concern given the distance and time elapsed, but stressed that he wasn't certain and that there just wasn't any real information other than their own speculation. It was an issue, just not an immediate one.

From that came the topic of radiation sickness, and then just sickness in general. That led to medical needs and the realization that they were pretty much on their own in that department. There were no doctors or dentists among them. There were a number of people trained in CPR and at least two people capable of stitching wounds and reading x-rays, though.

They talked about food, fuel, energy, water and how best to conserve them. What to do with the garbage. They talked about many things. Then Davis began to steer the conversation to where he wanted it to go.

He brought up the need for everyone to be capable of defending themselves. He brought up the notion that help may never arrive and that they should be prepared for the worst. That the days ahead could get darker than anyone could imagine. Davis worked the crowd into fervor and then laid it on them: his master plan, The Wall.

There were some scoffs, as was to be expected—it was a crazy idea, but these were crazy times—but there were more nods of approval than anything else. Some people left, and once one left, there were always followers, and they left too. Most of the people were on board with his idea to wall off the town, though, which made Davis very happy. He hadn't thought of what he would do or say if it turned out to be ill-favored. Davis smiled and began to wrap things up.

The meeting slowly came to an end. People had a lot of questions and probably just wanted to be out and talking to each other. It went as well as he could have expected, and starting tomorrow the planning would begin. Tomorrow at sunrise Davis would have a dozen or so people gathered at the station to help draw up the plans for the wall. They would scout for supplies and tools and begin to gather up what they would need to put the plan in motion.

That was tomorrow though, and right now Davis was needed at Mourningside to make sure the long dead stayed dead. He shook a few hands, then headed out in a hurry.

21 IF IT'S THE LAST THING WE EVER DO

Jon-Jon fumbled for words. "I know we have something...I'm not sure what exactly, but you know it's more than nothing."

"I know," Dawn said with a half smile.

"I don't think it's a good idea to stick around. This sheriff guy is out of his mind. You've seen what's around here—nothing but death and destruction. We need to get away, far the fuck away from all this."

"I don't want to stick around here any more than you do, but where can we go? Hmm, I mean seriously, this is all just fucked. Those things are everywhere. Dead people are everywhere, and anywhere we go there will be new people. At least we know these people." Her lip trembled.

"True, but...what if we go somewhere cold. Someplace where they can freeze, and you and me can get cozy by a fire." He smiled at her.

"That sounds great, but...but...how the hell can we get there? The roads are shit. We barely made it here and look how many lives we lost along the way. Do you really think the two of us can just drive off into the sunset?"

"Maybe. Once we get past Titan City we can head northwest, not even have to worry about New York and just head toward Canada?" Even as he said it he didn't fully believe that the two of them could do it on their own.

"It's crazy, maybe if we all went it could work. But we'd be dead long before the city. Just think about how many more of them there'll be in a big city like that. Whoever didn't burn up from the bombing is going to come back—a city of the dead--"

"Against the two of us," Jon-Jon cut her off, "they wouldn't stand--"

"We wouldn't even be a snack," she snapped. "We would get up, as dead as them, and come right back here looking for..." she broke off into tears.

Jon-Jon held her, but couldn't console her one bit. They cried in each others arms, unable to move. They would stay the course. They would help build the wall, and maybe, just maybe, they would survive.

***

"I want to go back home," Judy said.

"Me too, babe," Scott replied, "I don't see it happening, but I want to go back too."

"I miss Mister Butters so much," she began to weep. "I hope he's okay."

"I know, I know." He rubbed her back.

"Steamer's doing just fine on his own, he never needed us—it was the other way around," Scott said.

"Stop calling him that."

"It's his name," Scott smiled.

After a few quiet moments Judy said, "We'll never see our home again, will we? This is never going to end is it? We're all just going to die."

"It has to end. We can survive this. We just have to be smart about it. We got to keep our heads screwed on straight." Scott rubbed his forehead. "If you want to go back home we can try it. But I feel safer with everyone else. I think we stand a better chance together than we do on our own."

"Me too. I'd love to go back home, though, but you're right. We're safer together. Maybe this wall thing can work, too, right?"

"Sure it can. All we need is enough time to do it."

With that they felt more at ease. They felt hope begin to kindle again somewhere deep inside them.

22 RUNAWAYS

They were driving on fumes, and fast too. How they made it so far and managed to survive none of them knew. After Titan City had been leveled, and another after that, they knew they had to leave and get as far away as they could. They didn't know how, or to where, and a series of near-disasters on the road had led them to just outside of New Haven.

They had not rested, had not slept, and had only managed to drive by some form of autonomy. Everything that had gotten them to where they were was by accident or luck, and either of them would be hard-pressed to differentiate between the two.

Fighting to keep her eyelids open, Danni drove as fast as the car would allow her. She had with her two passengers: to her right, Clem, who was barely awake, and Darryl, the panicked back-seat driver who was practically sitting on her shoulder irritating the shit out of her. They came across him by sheer luck as well, and as the two in the front would agree, it was probably a bit of bad luck. The guy was bad news, drugged-out, annoying, and of little-to-no help at all.

Dane was on roadblock duty again. But apart from guarding the town line he was also to be doing some preliminary work on what would be the wall: and that meant digging, and Dane hated digging. He didn't go through the academy to dig ditches. He became a cop to stop bad guys and go on high-speed car chases. Little did he know that he would be giving out speeding tickets for most of the time leading up to the end of days.

Dane noticed the little car kicking up dust in the distance and whistled to Keith, who was also working the roadblock with him. Keith had a flask in one hand and a shovel in the other. He looked in the direction of Dane's finger and nodded, but didn't seem impressed. They didn't have many people coming through town lately, but he figured they would eventually.

They pulled themselves up out of the growing ditch, and readied themselves behind their cruisers. Dane stood ready with a rifle while Keith grabbed the handset to the car's PA system. The car was not slowing down.

"Stop the car," Keith slurred out.

They didn't.

"Stop the car," Keith yelled louder.

The car continued to speed forward. Dane was ready to fire.

"Stop the fucking car, or we will shoot," Keith screamed.

Dane fired at the front tire. Though not the best of shots, he hit his mark and caused the car to swerve violently. It didn't slow down however, and Dane and Keith had to run out of the way as it came crashing into the two cruisers.

The back-seat driver was thrown through the windshield, sending tiny cubes of bloodied glass into the air. He smacked his face on the cruiser and then lay limp on the hood of it. Danni had fallen asleep, and only after the impact of smashing into the two police cruisers did she stir from sleep. Her nose was broken on the steering wheel and blood poured from it—she was in a daze. Clem lay unconscious with his body slumped forward, after smacking his head against the dashboard. Had he not been wearing a seatbelt he'd probably have been thrown through the windshield with Darryl.

Dane rushed toward the car, slinging the rifle over his shoulder and pulling out his service weapon from his holster. Keith was right behind him.

"Don't fucking move," Dane commanded.

"Wha-wha- happened," Danni mumbled, her words soft around the edges.

"Dane," Keith tapped his shoulder.

"What is it," he turned.

The back-seat driver lifted himself from the hood of the cruiser. His jaw was slack and his face was mangled. He began to move, but Keith and Dane both fired at the dead man. They didn't have to check his pulse to know he wasn't alive. The dead things had a look to themselves that no living person could pull off, actor or not.

The noise of the gunshots jolted Danni and Clem, back to reality and out of their semi-unconsciousness. Danni began to scream, and Clem tried to figure out what the hell had transpired in the short amount of time since he'd fallen asleep.

"Oh, my God! What've you done, why did you kill him?" she screamed.

"Maam, calm down." Dane said to her. "He was already dead." Dane told her.

"Then why are you pointing the fucking gun at me?" She was screaming at him. "I don't believe you. Leave us alone!"

"You drove straight at us you dumb bitch." Keith stormed closer to her.

"Don't you talk to her like that you bastard," Clem yelled as he got out of the car, stumbling with a bloody forehead.

"Sir, do not move. Stay where you are and put your hands in the air."

"You gonna shoot him too? Shoot us both?"

"No way," Clem chimed in. "She's hurt and I'm hurt, and I'll be Goddamned if I'm going to let you two do anymore damage. Shoot me if you want, but I ain't gonna take yer shit."

"Listen old man, we don't want to hurt you. We told you to stop, but you guys kept driving. Look at it from our point of view—you tried to run us down!"

"Well we didn't mean to, I fell asleep and I guess Danni did to. We didn't mean it. We haven't slept, just been driving...seems like days. We don't have any real weapons, just a pipe and a baseball bat. Now I'm gonna get her out of the car. You two want to help or keep pointing your guns at us?"

They helped get the woman from the car. She was weak, and dizzy. Dane got them both some water. He sat with them by the side of the road as Keith called for back-up.

***

Sal, having slept enough to just barely function answered the call for back-up. When he arrived on the scene he saw Dane and Keith looking over their cruisers and spotted the two new arrivals to town.

He pulled over close to the two folks who sat off to the side. They looked at him with penetrating skeptical eyes. The type of eyes he had grown accustomed to since putting on the badge.

In Sal's experience most people didn't care much for cops unless they needed them. Even in a town like New Haven he still got the looks, less than he did before his move, but some were just nicer about it. Not these two, these two looked like they didn't even trust the wind or the sun.

He stepped over to the car and nodded to the two folks. He tried to smile and they didn't smile back.

"Hi there, you folks okay?"

"Been better," the man said.

"Been worse," said Danni.

"You mind me asking what happened here?"

"You just did," cracked the old man.

"Guess so. Well?"

"I guess I fell asleep at the wheel." Danni said. "Crashed into your friends over there—got our friend killed."

"Sorry about your friend, at least you two are okay, right?" Sal forced a smile. He couldn't care less about their friend, or about them. But since his brothers of the badge were okay he would try to keep his humanity, even if it was fading fast.

"It's okay," Clem said. "He wasn't exactly a friend, more like a pain in the ass. But he was alive for a bit and we'd rather travel with one of the living than one of the dead."

"Hmm," Sal nodded, unsure of what else to say. "Well, if you'll excuse me, I'm going to go see what the damage is." He walked over to Dane and Keith.

Keith stared at Sal with squinty eyes as he walked over to them. Dane was kneeling down looking under the car, trying to figure out what was leaking.

"Thank God it's Friday," Sal said.

"Shit, it's Friday already? I guess that means you brought us our checks," Keith smiled.

"Checks? Ever hear of direct deposit?"

Keith laughed. "I don't trust computers."

"What's the damage?"

"Well, this one's leaking something. Looks like coolant. And it's not turning over. The other's fine, besides the busted taillight. That guy's dead, and their car is totaled." Dane stood up and brushed off his pants.

"Yep, he looks dead all right," Sal smirked.

"Had no idea New Haven was such a tourist destination. Maybe we should get cracking on this wall, so we can keep people out—especially if their crashing in like this." Sal chuckled.

"Don't get me started on that fucking wall bullshit," Keith slurred.

They all had a good laugh, though Keith really didn't think this wall was a great idea. He felt it was a joke that he just didn't get. Sal and Dane were on board with it, but knew it was a huge undertaking; maybe more than they could handle. The two sitting off to the side didn't seem to appreciate the laughter.

"Clem, what're you thinking?" Danni whispered.

"Thinking about my sweet Lorraine," he replied.

"I know you are. But what about these people?"

"They seem okay I guess—they're breathing air, right? What more do you want from them?"

"I dunno. They just seem to be taking this all so lightly."

"Maybe that's how they cope with it. But we've been cooped up and removed from the reality of things for a long time. These guys seem like they've been on the front lines the whole time. Just look at all the remains."

Danni hadn't noticed it before, but once she began to pay attention to her surroundings she noticed all sorts of human remains scattered around. Just a few feet away from where they sat lied a crumbled up pile of ash and bone. The dust and dirt covered it like camouflage—she looked around at the landscape and shivered at the number of bones she spotted. Clem was right, she thought. She had been removed from the world. She was a stranger to it now, and she wasn't sure if she wanted to get to know it.

23 UNREST

West Virginia.
Mount Weather Special Facility.

Rachel rubbed her temples firmly and slowly. Her head ached, her neck hurt, and grabbing a nap on the cot in the break room didn't do her any favors. She fished around in her bag and pulled out a bottle of aspirin. She twisted the top off and shook three of the little white tablets into the palm of her hand, popped them into her mouth and swallowed. She didn't need anything to chase them down, but opened a can of cola anyway. She drank it for the sugar and the caffeine more than anything. Rachel wasn't much for sodas but she figured it couldn't hurt, it was the end of the world anyway—a few calories weren't going to kill her, at least she hoped.

She tilted her head back and emptied the last mouthful of bubbly cola into her mouth. She swished the fluid around in her mouth, then gulped it down. Taking aim at a wastebasket in the far corner she launched the empty can. It hit the floor about four feet shy, filling the room with a clank and then a scuttle. Rachel snapped her fingers in mock disappointment and headed for the door.

She was once again suited up and ready to continue her work with the cadaver. A new guard was in the same spot as the old one, who nodded at her as she entered the room. She nodded back.

She attempted to feed the creature the cold strips of flesh, but even as they dangled over its dry, cracked lips the thing wanted nothing to do with it. She tried heating the flesh, but the soldier still wouldn't take it into his mouth. She tried asking him more questions but the guttural noises when played back were just that: noises.

It left her with still more questions, and a few that questioned her own sanity. But when she replayed the previous session, the words were there. She couldn't go to her colleagues or superiors unless she had more to show them. She thought maybe she'd have better luck with a fresher specimen. She left the room, dissatisfied but with a sense diligence.

She went to the large lab room full of specimens and limbs and she obtained more chunks of flesh.

"Hi," she said to the lab technician seated at the main station. "Is it possible to get a fresher specimen?"

"Hey. What do you mean by 'fresher'? They all kind of have an odor—they're rotting corpses."

"Obviously. I'm looking for something that hasn't been deceased too long. Maybe something came in that just died?" She sounded a little too hopeful, even for herself.

"Give me a second, and let me check the charts." The technician turned his attention to his computer monitor.

He scrolled through a long list of specimens. The list was sorted by date received. Looking at the last entry and clicking on it opened a corresponding file that contained all available information about the specimen.

"We got this one, came in yesterday; Private First Class Nick Henshaw. Problem is Doctor Tran already has him, says Henshaw died yesterday in the observation unit and Tran nabbed him only a few hours later. He's the freshest thing we got."

"Great, Tran isn't going to give him up. Any chance you can notify me if anything comes in that's been recently deceased?"

"Sure thing. I can't promise anything, but if it comes in on my watch it's all yours. You might want to see if Tran will share with you: he's got to sleep and eat sometime," He said, smiling.

"Thanks, but I think Tran might be a vampire. And he seems to like talking to dead people over us living types," she replied.

Despite her gut feelings about Doctor Tran, Rachel decided to see if it was possible for him to allow her some access to his specimen. They were colleagues after all, and after the same thing. But Rachel felt that Tran might not see things that way. This was also a huge opportunity to save all of humankind, and what person—especially a doctor—would not want to be the responsible individual? Rachel knew she would love to be the one, if only to end the long days and longer nights.

She found the room where he was stationed. There was a similar guard stationed outside the room looking in, and Doctor Tran was inside. He was sawing open the top of the creature's head. The fast whirring sound of the saw filled the room.

Rachel stood next to the guard and waited. She didn't want to enter the room while he was performing such a task. She would expect the same courtesy if the situation were reversed, and she hoped he would appreciate the gesture.

The noise ended, Doctor Tran shut off the saw, laying it down on a small stainless steel tray. He then held onto the creatures head with the tips of his fingers and began to pry off the top portion of the specimen's head. Though Rachel couldn't hear it, she knew it was creating a schhllluck-like noise, similar to the sound of suction. Tran placed the top of the head onto the same tray where the saw lay. When he turned back around he finally noticed Rachel looking into the room. He simply cocked his head at her, surprised to see her standing there.

He walked to the door, opened it and a made an overly dramatic and gentlemanly bow, extending his free arm in a gesture for her to come inside. She smiled, and entered the room.

"To what to I deserve this pleasure?"

"Well, Doctor Tran, I was wondering if I may borrow your cadaver."

"Please, call me Gregory. And as you can see my cadaver and I are in the middle of something." He gestured to the creature with its brain exposed and glistening in the lab's diffused light.

"Yes, Gregory. I was hoping that maybe in your down time I can examine him. Perhaps when you go for lunch or sleep?"

"And what would you be doing with him?" Tran seemed almost as if he already knew the answer.

"Just doing a cursory examination," she replied coldly.

"Don't you mean an interrogation?" Tran smiled, his small eyes gleaming.

"What do you mean Doc...Gregory?"

"Come on Rachel. You're a smart girl, I'm a borderline genius and we both know why you want to see this particular specimen. The reason: because he's fresh!" He emphasized every letter of the word 'fresh', almost sounding like a snake.

"You're right Doctor--"

"Gregory, please. There is no need for formalities—it is the end of the world Rachel, we may as well be janitors. You and I are on to something. You may be a day late and a dollar short, but I'll give you the dollar. And I'll let you speak to my dead friend over here who I'm sure has plenty to tell you." He sounded almost mad. But he wasn't mad: he was excited—enthralled.

Rachel was taken aback by Tran's bluntness and willingness to share. She had been totally wrong about him and now felt foolish. "Would you mind telling me what you mean Gregory?"

"Still with the games, I see."

"No games. Let's talk."

"Fine, then let's talk out of these suits and with a cup of tea." He exited the room.

***

Rachel and Doctor Tran sat in the break room. Tran rhythmically dipped his tea bag in and out of his cup of steaming hot water. The water grew cloudier with every dunk. Rachel had another can of cola. It was cold, fizzy, and just as refreshing as the one she had earlier.

"I'm assuming at this point you've discovered that these things can in fact communicate?"

Rachel nodded.

"Okay, good, good. I discovered it on day one—quite accidentally, but regardless I did. It was nothing more than a few words, spoken backward, and hard to make out. It really didn't tell me anything we hadn't already figured out at this point: basically that they are hungry and want flesh, that much is obvious."

Rachel stared at Tran. She was fixated on every syllable that fell from his lips. He was being dramatic and stringing her along, and she wanted badly to be able to press a fast forward button and speed up to the stuff she didn't already know herself. But she couldn't. So he kept talking, and she kept listening.

"I've found out that not every one of the cadavers are capable of communicating. Maybe they are too far gone. Whatever the reason is, it doesn't matter. The trick I've found out—which is what you would have learned on your own—is to find the freshest specimen possible. And by freshest I mean those who have recently reanimated, not the ones who've been dead for days."

He paused to take a sip of tea and then continued, "I assume the condition of the specimen can also be of importance in the same regard." Tran began to speak quietly. "Also, it appears that whatever allows for the ability to communicate degenerates over time, quickly I might add, and never comes back. They are still able to 'speak' to some extent, but no exchange is possible."

"So, you're saying we have a small window of time where we can talk to the dead, and they can talk back?"

"Exactly! Though, I must warn you, the speech is basic, and vague, and they have difficulty understanding complicated sentences."

"Let me ask you this: Do they remember who they are?"

"Yes. From what I've gathered they are who they were in life. Only now they speak of being trapped in a darkness, controlled by hunger. Very vague statements, but statements nonetheless." Tran stopped dunking his tea bag and sipped, allowing Rachel the time to absorb his words.

Rachel was shocked to hear the answer to her question. It pained her deeply to know the answer and feared how others would handle that knowledge. If people knew their loved ones were still inside those dead husks, would they be able to dispatch them to survive? She didn't think so.

"Why haven't you told anyone this?"

"I tried to, but it was dismissed as nonsense. I was threatened with being removed from the premises unless I focused on the task at hand—stopping the dead from coming back."

"Jesus," Rachel said, unable to understand why their superiors wouldn't be interested in the knowledge. It's not like Doctor Tran is a crackpot—he's one of the elite. He wasn't kidding in the slightest when he said, 'borderline genius,' if anything, he was being modest by adding borderline.

"They are close-minded fools. Their only concern seems to be pinning the bombings on some terrorist-harboring country even remotely capable of committing the act. When in reality who is ever going to know?" Tran grew angry.

"Pinning?" Rachel asked.

Tran looked perplexed. "Come on Rachel, please don't tell me you think anyone except our government dropped those bombs?"

"Those are American cities! They couldn't have," she protested, but had already considered it a possibility.

"They did. It's all strategy—just a group of pieces on a chessboard—nothing more. And it makes perfect sense. I understand why it needs to be done, but why worry about an excuse? Is there anyone reporting this? No! Of course not."

"No, can't be…that can't be true," she whimpered. She wanted to hold onto her idealistic view of the world she once knew. From a military perspective it made perfect sense to eliminate the places that harbored the largest numbers of hostiles first. Even in painting you did your broad strokes first, then went in and did the detail work as means of a finish.

After they talked some more, Tran left her to fetch a few hours of sleep and relinquished his cadaver to her. Rachel wasted no time in examining the specimen and hearing for herself what the creature had to say. It didn't say much, and much of what it did say she had already heard from Tran. But hearing it from the horse's mouth was an entirely different experience.

The dead soldier, with its brain exposed, was once a man with feelings, dreams, and aspirations. He had a family and people who cared for him, and people he cared for in return. And Rachel could hear his garbled pleas for release, for flesh, and it sickened her right down to her bones.

What she had learned in the few hours she spent with the soldier was that the consummation of living flesh helped ease the pains of living death. And that there was no light waiting for her at the end of her life, just a darkness waiting to envelop her.

She ran her hand along the cadaver's cold arm. She could feel the hardened veins through the thick material of the suit. She looked the dead man in the eyes, feeling sorry for him. He was in there, staring through a darkness he didn't understand, unable to fight his urges for flesh. For whatever reason, unable to rest.

24 SURVIVORS

Sal left Dane and Keith where they were. One of the cruisers worked well enough, and they had plenty of time left on their shift. They'd continue with the ditch-digging, no doubt griping about it the entire time, and hoped to have the rest of their shift go by incident-free. They both held their breath.

Danni and Clem sat in the back of Sal's cruisers. They looked filthy and disheveled and on the verge of collapse. Sal continually looked at them from the rear view mirror to make sure neither of them turned into a flesh eater. He had asked them if either of them had been bitten, and they both said 'no', but by the looks of them they could've been dead already.

Sal pulled up to the station, parked, and opened the back door for his two passengers. They got out with much effort, exhaustion taking its toll on them, and followed him inside.

Sal led them through the desolate station to the large meeting room where the map and the tacks remained from the last time he was in there. He offered them coffee or water, and they accepted gratefully. They sat in the room staring at the map, curious as to what all the colored pushpins represented.

Once Sal returned with their drinks and an added bonus of some stale cookies he informed them of what the different colored pins stood for. Sal asked them if they could add any to the map, but they declined.

"You'd be out of pins," Clem said, munching on a crunchy cookie.

"Well, if you want to add a few, by all means, go ahead," Sal suggested, waving his hand across the map.

Clem and Danni nodded, too busy stuffing their faces to respond with words.

"You two just sit tight for a bit till the Sheriff shows up. He wants to talk to you two, should be here in a few. If you want more to drink or eat, the pantry is right around that bend." He pointed and said, "First door on the left—help yourself."

"I think we might," Danni said. "Thank you."

Sal smiled, and left the room. Clem stared at the map and decided to add a few more tacks. Once he was done, he pictured connecting the dots with an imaginary red line. The line made a crooked trail to New Haven.

Danni pinched her nose softly. It was tender to the touch and swollen, as were parts of her face. Her front teeth were somewhat numb feeling, but felt firmly in place—she was thankful for that much.

She got up and began to wander around, hoping to find the ladies room. She found the pantry, grabbed another cookie, and continued to wander. She eventually found the ladies room, and looked at herself in the mirror. She remembered the last time she found herself in a new place looking into a mirror and trying to figure out who was looking back at her.

This time she had no clue. She couldn't recognize the woman looking back at all. She was hardened, with tight lips and sunken eyes, dirty skin, oily hair, thick eyebrows and not a trace of make-up. The end of the world didn't do her looks any justice. She looked like a scrawny Sigourney Weaver from the Aliens movies but without the strong will, and the nerves of steel. She looked as dead as the things she ran from, and she was just as hungry.

She cleaned herself off in the sink as best she could. And when she returned her eyes to the mirror her appearance wasn't much better. She flipped herself the bird and left the room.

Left alone, Clem had fallen asleep in his chair. His head hung back and to the right, and any second he would start to snore. Danni didn't wake him. She just sat next to him and crossed her arms over her chest, put her head down and quickly joined him. In the span of a few minutes they were both snoring. They managed about twenty minutes of sleep before Sheriff Davis came in and dropped his notepad on the table, and pulled up a chair.

"Morning," Davis said sarcastically.

Danni lifted her head up and with squinty eyes replied, "its morning already?"

"Might as well be," Davis said.

Danni nudged Clem, who still hadn't woken up, on the arm. He'd never been a deep sleeper, but lately he'd been able to sleep through just about anything.

"Whuh—Oh! Hey," Clem said groggily, wiping drool from the corner of his mouth.

"Now that you're both up, I'm just going to cut to the chase. If you're staying in town, I need to know your names and what you can do. If you can't do anything then you can leave. Every one who stays in New Haven does something for New Haven."

"I can respect that," Clem said. "But I'm not sure what use I can be. I've had every shit job under the sun, but I ain't getting any younger." He looked genuinely saddened by his own words. "Name's Clem."

Danni rubbed his arm gently as he spoke, staring at Davis. She felt like she was being judged. "I'm Danielle—everyone calls me Danni, though. There's not much I can do. I was going to school—didn't really know what I wanted to do, and now it doesn't matter."

"So I should put you down for nothing?" Davis asked.

"I'll try to do whatever it is you want from me," she replied, hoping any request would be within reason, and hoping the world wasn't as dark as the back of her mind.

"Can you dig ditches and learn how to shoot?"

"Sounds easy enough," Danni replied.

"Good, you'll start tomorrow."

"Okay."

"Clem... I take it with all your shit jobs over the years you've learned how to be handy?"

"I'd say so. I'm no MacGyver, but I get by all right," he managed.

"Good, same deal—you'll start tomorrow. Both of you rest up today. Eat, drink, and clean yourselves up. I'll see if I can get you both some clothes and a decent dinner. Till then have at whatever's lying around. There're holding cells in the back, feel free to get some sleep in one of them till we can find you both something a bit more permanent," he said as he stood up to leave.

"Thanks, uh...," Clem muttered.

"Bruce—Bruce Davis," he said, and then walked out.

"Thanks Bruce," Clem said, still with a sad look etched into his face.

***

Davis brought clothes and dinner for his latest guests. They were grateful, and showed him as much by attacking the foil-wrapped plates with a ferocious hunger usually only seen by the dead things stalking the earth. Davis wanted to laugh, but choked it back and replaced it with something closer to sorrow.

Davis apologized for taking so long, but with all the running around he was doing he couldn't be bothered by thinking of dinner, and certainly not anyone else's. They figured he forgot, but were happy to see him show up with two plates full of food—even if it was hours past any respectable dinnertime… and cold.

His face wore the beatings of the day and he didn't try to hide it. He fell asleep in the chair, and Clem and Danni didn't notice till they had licked their plates clean and sucked the remains from their fingertips. They let him catch a nap while they took a closer look at the clothes. Danni left to put hers on, and after a second thought, Clem did the same. He'd hate for the sheriff to wake up and catch an eyeful of Clem's old ball bag.

25 DEAD RECKONING

New Haven.
The next day.

Dane had a few hours before he was due to report to Davis. He and Susan remained comfortably entwined on the bed and in between the sheets. Cher, the little cute and cuddly mutt that she was, sat at the foot of the bed as usual. She watched them with fond disinterest.

Dane rubbed Susan's lower back and kissed her shoulder. She moaned with that sleepy soft voice she so often woke up with. She rubbed his hand, eager to relive last night's brief but still-damn-good escapade, and Dane took it as invitation to something more. He leaned in closer to her, leaving a trail of soft kisses from her shoulder to her neck. She giggled once he got to her earlobe: she always did, and Dane loved it. His free arm reached up her side, slithering ever closer to her breast as his mouth found his way to hers, and just before he could start to work her nipple she turned her head.

"Ugh, morning breath," she groaned.

"Real nice," Dane replied.

"If you want any more of this," she spun around, "you're going to brush your teeth and get into the shower, before I change my mind."

Usually Dane would argue, or put up a fight, or just throw her down till she herself wanted it bad enough to put up with the bad breath or the stench of a long day. But these days were different.

He hopped out of bed with a bounce in his body that could only be brought on the by the promise of sex. He tossed his shirt off and to the floor as he headed to the bathroom. He grabbed his toothbrush and went to work.

"You could use some brushing too bee-yotch," he said as he brushed his teeth.

She joined him, and like a dog he began to hump her leg. She put up with it, allowing him to grow hard, as a dribble of foamy toothpaste fell from his mouth. A spit and a rinse later they were both in the shower feeling each other up. Dane rubbed his hard prick against her leg as he worked her clit with his other hand. She held his hand firmly as his fingers probed deep inside her and each time he was about to pull out she'd force his fingers back inside. He stopped rubbing his member against her leg and grabbed her breast. He grabbed it hard and pinched the nipple so it stood at full attention. Susan spun around and grabbed his prick, soaping it up and working his balls as he kissed her neck and sucked on her nipples.

They worked each other hard till they were both about ready to burst. Then Susan spun around again, giving Dane her back. Being careful not to slip, Dane eased his member into Susan. She took all of him, moaning and sliding back, sticking her ass up. Dane pushed back, gripping the slope of her hips. They both moaned and grunted, giving and taking. Susan kept pushing back harder, her pussy started to throb. She gripped her breasts tight, kissing her nipples as Dane slid in and out. Susan let out an orgasmic scream, unable to hold out any longer Dane followed behind. They both bucked and trembled as they came together, every movement a tremor.

They came down from their sexual high together, kissing softly under the quickly cooling water as Dane's cum trickled down her leg, spiraling down the drain.

***

Eddie scribbled his thoughts into his spiral bound notebook of a journal. He tried to write in it as often as possible, but the last few days had been so hectic he hadn't even given it a thought. Today was the first day in a long time he could remember where he awoke calmly, and had some time to think instead of just react. He thought about all he'd seen over the last few days and wrote it down, hoping in some way that it would make more sense on paper than it did in his head—it didn't of course, but he hoped it might.

Janice pretended to sleep. She had slept some during the night, not much, but some. She peeked through her nearly closed eyelids watching over her two boys—Eddie, as he wrote, and Joseph as he snored. Joseph could sleep through anything, she thought, just like his father. Her eyes started to tear with the thought of him and she squeezed them shut tight.

***

Scott and Judy walked around the grounds of the VFW hall trying to recapture a bit of their former routine. They were walkers, walked in the morning, after lunch, and in the evening. Anytime they could set their feet to pavement and make them move they did. This morning was no exception. The sky was a mix of magenta and morning blue with swirls of torn-cotton-like clouds being pulled parallel to the horizon. The breeze was cool, if only a bit putrid, and gently pushed the blades of grass as it swept through the landscape.

They didn't talk much, but walked hand in hand. There wasn't much to say, and the quiet was a welcome change of pace compared to the last few weeks, and the last few days in particular. Scott looked around, taking in the parts of the world that were still full of life: the trees, the sky, the leaves that were beginning to change. The birds were still beautiful and didn't seem to mind humankind facing their darkest days. They chirped as if spreading the news—'Did you hear? Man's time is at an end.' Scott grew angry at the thought. Fucking birds, what did they know? Scott thought about how easy life could've been if he'd had wings: he could've just flown away when life got hard.

Judy stopped walking and gripped Scott's hand tightly.

"Shit," she said, "look, up by those trees!"

Scott looked toward the tree line, just up the hill. "Is that the only one?"

"Can't tell." Judy scoured the tree line for more of the deaders.

"It looks like its just standing there," Scott commented. Then he noticed that it was moving, just very slowly.

"Let's go tell the others," Judy said.

"Fuck that! Let's go blow its brains out." He walked forward, pulling Judy.

"Come on. I think you're starting to like this shit," Judy said.

146

"Like it? Really? Judy, that's bullshit. I just don't think we need to tell everyone that there's one dead guy up the hill when we can take care of it ourselves. How many of these things have we killed on our own?"

"A lot, but still—it doesn't mean you have to like it."

"I don't like it, now stop saying that. It makes me feel like a creep or something."

"You are a creep," she smiled.

"Ha ha, very funny."

As they walked closer to the dead thing, it noticed them and stumbled away from the tree line. It nearly fell as it shambled down the side of the hill, stepping out from behind the long shadows of the trees.

"Damn! I can smell him from here," Judy complained, waiving her hand in front of her face.

"Yep, we got a ripe one." He pulled a handgun from his waistline.

Scott took a firing stance. He had enough time to aim his shot properly as the deader stumbled closer. He fired, and the dead thing fell. Scott walked closer to it, the gun in front.

"Scott! Get back here!" Judy screamed.

Scott spun around to look at her as she stood with one hand over her mouth and the other pointing at the tree line. Scott followed her finger up the hill, and staggered backward as hundreds of deader things shambled out from the shadows of the woods.

"Holy fuck," he said, and ran toward Judy.

They both ran screaming down the hill and back toward the VFW hall. The dead things followed in their slow meandering way.

The deader Scott shot stumbled to its feet, unimpressed by the man's aim, and rejoined the horde of dead that staggered down the hill. Many of them were naked and burned—all were grotesque. The morning sun lit the hillside beautifully. It would've been picturesque if not for the dead things shambling through the tall, lime-green grass, some dragging intestines gone black and leathery. On top of the hill, from out of the shadows of the trees staggered many more. In only a few short moments the hill was covered with the living dead.

The doors of the VFW hall burst open as Scott shouldered through them with Judy right behind him.

"We've got to get out of here and get the Sheriff!" Scott yelled.

"What's going on?" Dawn asked, half asleep and stumbling to her feet.

"No time—everyone out! Deaders everywhere," Scott hollered.

"Hundreds of them, coming from the woods," Judy panted.

"Fuck! Fuck! Fuck!" Joseph grumbled as he too shook off sleep, along with everyone else.

Eddie and his mother looked at each other. Eddie wrapped his arm around her shoulder and made for the door, escorting her out. Joseph followed behind, grabbing whatever stuff they had lying about. Frankie ran for the door, shotgun in hand as Scott and Judy held the doors open, continuing to yell.

By the time Frankie made it outside, the dead things were halfway toward the hall. Frankie didn't have time to think, only to act. He ran toward the shambling dead, standing between them and the row of vehicles.

Eddie rushed his mother into their car, started it and moved forward. He popped the trunk, and he and Joseph grabbed what guns they could and ran to Frankie's side. They began to take shots at the creatures, but only when they could make them count. Their hands were shaky, but after firing a few rounds their nerves solidified and their aim improved.

***

Sal was riding around town, slowly driving through his old route when he heard what sounded like gunshots. It had to be gunshots he thought, what else could it be? He pressed down a little harder on the gas and poked his head out the window more, as if it would help him hear things better. He heard the noise again, and again. He was indeed hearing gunshots. He drove toward the direction of the noise, and had a good hunch about where they were coming from anyway.

As he approached the VFW hall, he could see the dead things coming from the woods and down the hill. They were everywhere. The morning sun highlighted their ghastly wounds, illuminating the gore in a golden glow.

"Calling all units, calling all units—requesting immediate assistance at the Hillside VFW. Bring anything and anyone…the shit has hit the fan," Sal squawked over the ham radio.

He drove his cruiser right up the lawn. Remembering Dane's unsuspecting bravado from a few days ago, Sal revved his cruiser up and plowed right through a good dozen or so of the deaders. Casting even more of them to the ground. Two of them clung to the underside of the cruiser, their limbs growing mangled under the steel chassis of the vehicle. He put the cruiser in reverse and spun his way through a few more. He heard the punishing sounds of flesh denting his cruiser and knew the cruiser wouldn't be able to continue running the dead things down. If he didn't break an axle, the suspension would surely go, and if not that, then something else would find a way of breaking.

"Hell yeah!" Joseph shook his fist in excitement.

Frankie hollered at the storm of oncoming dead as he fired and pumped and repeated. He stood his line in the field and knew the others at his side would do the same. They knew their positions in the ragtag chain of command: some ran to the vehicles in preparation to hightail it, others saw to the children, some gathered the goods and weapons, while others saw to the bloody details of dispatching man's ever present shadow of death.

They wouldn't be able to fight them off much longer, however. Their sheer numbers were more than anything they had ever seen–far more than they had come across on the road, and certainly more than at the school. They were more than an army–they were a sea, and eventually even the best of swimmers will die in the ocean if stuck there long enough.

With Janice somewhat-safely in her car, Eddie ran to his brother's side with his weapon drawn. Eddie took a breath, picked a target, and fired. The anxiety left his body and coursed through the barrel of his gun as a bullet. He hit his mark, it was far from a perfect shot, but it was good enough. The dead things head slumped back, and the rest of its body collapsed, tripping up a couple of the creatures behind it.

"Eddie, you know what this reminds me of?" Joseph asked.

"Reminds me of staying up late to watch scary movies, only about a million times worse," Eddie replied, firing another shot.

"No, it reminds me of when we used to shoot our G.I. Joe's with rubber band guns–remember those?"

"I don't remember having this many G.I. Joe's," Eddie replied.

Frankie looked over to the two brothers. "Are you guys really talking about G.I. Joe's right now?"

"Yeah," they both replied.

"I love G.I. Joe's! Snake-Eyes was the shit!" Frankie smiled, sweat dripping down his cheek.

"Shit yeah he was," Joseph said, "He'd fuck these things up," he continued.

"We gotta move back," Scott yelled. "They're getting too fucking close!"

They moved back. They were only steps away from the vehicles, which were ready to roll out with extremely eager drivers waiving them to get in. They continued to hold their ground, barely making a dent in the number of walking dead.

Sal took another swipe into the crowd of dead, pummeling them with the front of his cruiser, leaving tread marks all through the field. His cruiser was almost completely covered in blood and gore, like a Halloween prop at a haunted hayride. He continued to yell for backup over the radio, but no one was responding.

One of the bodies rolled up onto the windshield, hitting it hard enough to crack the glass. Sal didn't hear it crack, but once another rolled up and over he could see it begin to splinter. He spun the wheel around trying to deflect the dead away from the windshield and kicked up bloodied earth as he sped away, only to hit another few on his way away from the horde.

The dead thing rolled up the hood and into the windshield, its head the straw that broke the camel's back. Sal screamed as the dead thing broke through the grass. He squirmed for his service weapon as the deader raised its arms, reached through the windshield and dragged itself closer. Its mouth began to move, chewing on the air and its own swollen lips.

Sal could smell its decaying blue-grey skin which was now coming over the steering wheel as he pulled up his handgun. He flipped the safety, loaded the barrel and stuck the gun to the dead things head and pulled the trigger. The black-blood blew back and spattered over Sal's entire face. It got into his eyes, and mouth and Sal frantically wiped it off and spat it out.

"Fuck," he yelled, and fired at another deader that began to crawl into the opening.

Sal could no longer see where he was going, but he continued to keep his foot pressed to the floor. He fired again, taking the face off of the new intruder and feeling its cold blood blow back onto his face. He didn't know how he knew it, but he knew he was fucked.

***

Davis heard the crackling of the ham radio and was startled to wake. He couldn't make out much more than 'backup' and 'VFW', but that was all he needed. He couldn't tell whose voice it was, but figured it was Sal. He grabbed his pants from the floor, pulled them and jumped into his boots and headed out the door pulling over his shirt. His truck kicked up a cloud of dust as he sped over to the hall.

"Backup is on the way," Davis called over the ham. "I repeat: backup is on the way." Davis depressed the button again, "all units convene at the VFW immediately."

***

Susan shook Dane awake when she heard Davis's voice over the walkie-talkie. His eyes cracked open, but they didn't register anything other than bright lights and Susan's blurry face.

"Wh-what?" Dane mumbled, too asleep to realize that something was wrong.

"It's Davis," she said. "He's calling for backup at the VFW."

"Shit. Really?"

"Yeah. You gonna go?"

"Of course. I have to."

"You don't have to," she said. "We can just leave."

"Don't start that again. We've already gone over this. Where would we go?"

"I don't know, anywhere."

"Yeah, maybe tomorrow...watch out." He got up from the bed.

"Dane, I got a bad feeling about this," she said softly.

"Babe, please, don't start with that either. Its way too early and I haven't had any coffee--"

"Don't just dismiss me like that. I got a feeling, you know, like when my Grandma would get them. I just know this is bad...I don't want you to go...please...for me..."

"And do what? If I don't go we have to pick up and leave--I'd never be able to show my face around here again," Dane said, considering it.

"Fine, we'll go. I don't care. The world we knew doesn't exist anymore, so why should your job?"

Dane stared at her. Both of them were glassy-eyed, and he couldn't think of an answer, "they're my friends--"

"No. No, they're not."

"Yeah, Susan, some of them are."

"Are they friends worth dying for?"

***

Jon-Jon grabbed Dawn by the arm and raced the van. His heart thumped in his chest almost as rapidly as it did the moment he'd first seen a dead man get up and walk. But this was different--it was overwhelming, like a bad dream of being lost at sea and the boat just out of arm's reach. He wasn't going to let the boat speed away. He was getting on board and getting away as fast as he could.

He yelled to others to do the same, but no one could hear him over the several layers of panic-stricken screams and ear-shattering gunshots. Dawn could barely hear him, could barely believe that he was running away from the fight instead of to it. But she could tell from the way his lips parted and his eyes shimmered what he was saying.

Dawn turned in all directions, looking for someone to pull along with her, for someone to help. But everyone was either on their way to a vehicle or running with weapon in hand toward the dead attackers. Then she saw Yussef from the corner of her eye fall to the ground.

The little boy was scared pale, and spewing tears from his eyes. Dawn screamed for him to come and, by sheer luck, they caught eyes, because Yussef wouldn't have been able to make out her call amid the noise otherwise. But he knew enough to pick himself up and run toward her, and he ran as fast as thin little legs could carry him.

Dawn pulled Jon-Jon's arm hard, slowing him down long enough for Yussef to catch up. She grabbed his delicate wrist and pulled him close and the three of them ran toward the van.

Sal lost control of his cruiser and spun into Eddie's vehicle with Janice inside. She was thrown forward, hitting her head and nearly losing consciousness. Sal hit the car on the opposite side of where she sat. The impact was hard and hard enough to wreck the front axle.

In the crash Sal managed to pin one of the dead things between the two vehicles. He shook his head and stumbled out of the car. Noticing the dead thing trying to free itself made him laugh. His eyes grew wild, fierce, and his smile was as savage as the heart that now beat vengefully in his chest. He stepped over to it, reloading his handgun and laughing.

"Oh, you fuckers got me good, I'll give you that," he said. "I guess it makes perfect sense--death always wins, but I had hope." Sal hovered over the dead thing. "I'd hoped to live long enough to see the world get back to normal, but I guess dying's as normal as it's going to get."

Sal put the tip of the gun to the dead thing as it squirmed to get free. It hissed and reached and squirmed, but it didn't matter. Sal squeezed the trigger and the dead man's head erupted, spraying bits of gore as the bullet exited the back of its head.

By the time Sal turned around he was surrounded by a few of the creatures. One bit down on his shoulder and began to tear off clothing and flesh as Sal registered them. He screamed and pushed the filthy, rotten thing to the ground. He kicked it again, stomping on its chest and fired at its face. The things cheek ripped off and dropped to the dirt. He fired again, into the head and it moved no more.

He walked closer to the others and fired accordingly. Stepping uncomfortably close every time and putting them down one by one. Janice looked on in horror through the blood-streaked glass of the driver's side window. Her lip trembled but that was all she could give. She died inside when the horror hit home and was only living for the sake of her son's sanity. Once Sal dispatched the nearby-dead he walked over to her.

"You okay?" Sal asked.

"Good enough," she replied.

"Got a smoke?"

"I quit years ago," she said. "It's bad for your health." She tried to smile.

Sal laughed and turned back around. He walked toward the undead horde that staggered down the hillside.

Janice got out of the car. She was still a little dizzy but quickly got her bearings and headed over to her sons.

Sheriff Bruce Davis arrived as fast as he could. He sped up the small hill to the side of the VFW and saw the mayhem instantly. He didn't know where to focus and as he stepped out of his truck and had no idea where he was going. There was too much going on and he'd never seen anything this bad, or on such a scale. He'd been involved in small riots before, but they were nothing like this. They were chaotic, sure, but when you had a dozen or so trained officers in riot gear it was controllable, and this was anything but controllable.

"Everybody clear the area!" Davis screamed.

He walked toward the line of vehicles. Jon-Jon had just reached his van and was about to take off, but when he heard Davis yelling to do so the guilt that was building subsided. Jon-Jon drove off kicking up a cloud dirt behind him. Davis continued down the lineup calling out to 'clear the area,' and those smart enough to listen did so.

Davis then turned his attention to the hillside. He tried to take in the scene, but everything moved too rapidly. There was no time to think: he couldn't act but only react. His eyes focused on Sal. Sal was the first friend he'd made upon becoming sheriff and through it all they had remained friends. What was left of Davis's heart hardened in that spitfire split-second of a moment when he figured out that his friend was covered in blood and looked only a shade livelier than the dead things around. He was laughing like a lunatic and making gunshot noises with his mouth as his weapon clicked empty over and over again. The dead things began to surround them.

"Sal!" he screamed, running over to him. "What the fuck are you doing?" But Sal didn't answer. "Get away from them," he yelled as he drew closer.

Sal turned to look at his friend: not his boss, but his friend. He smiled, but the smile was broken to pieces as his laughter turned to sobs. He raised the gun to his head and held it there as the dead things came upon him. He gave one last cartoonish P-Choo as they dragged him to the ground screaming.

"No!"

By the time Davis was close enough to help his friend the deaders were pulling out foot after foot of his bloody, ropey innards. They pulled, fighting like hungry rats over subway scraps dropped by carefree yuppies. He couldn't scream anymore, but his face writhed in pain, the veins in his neck bulged but disappeared as they ripped the skin from it. One of the creatures bit his lip, tearing it down to the butt of his chin, exposing his coffee-stained teeth.

"No! You bastards! Get off him! Get off him," Davis cried.

He stood just behind the feasting dead and began to fire. His aim was off and his shots ran wild. He hit one in the neck, another in the back, another in the leg. He fought his emotions, and tried to force them down deep, but they wouldn't budge. Much like the dead, he couldn't keep them down.

He stepped closer, seeing more of his friend than he could handle and lost himself in a blind rage. He fired again, and again, and by some form of autonomy his shots connected so that all that was left was a pile of dead bodies with one coming back in the middle–Sal.

"No," the words fell like whispers but hurt worse than broken bones. "No, Sal…oh, God…oh…God…" He hesitated for a breath, then he shot him in the head. The pile again laid still.

Janice had found her way to her sons. They stood feet ahead of her and had no idea she was behind them. She watched on in mild disbelief, her boys now men and doing what they needed to do to survive.

They were two among several, Chuck was there with his fading tan and bleached out hair. He was a horrible shot and probably wasted bullets if anything, but his presence alone was comfort to others who held the line with him. She saw Frankie, his once youthful face now bore the scars of hard times, sleepless nights, and heavier than lead thoughts. She could barely recognize these men as the boys they were only weeks ago. Time flies, she thought, wondering if hers was up. She stared at the dead stumbling from the tree line. They still came in droves, staggering one crooked step at a time. Her eyes locked onto a small girl, and her thoughts flashed back to her daughter. In a flash she relived the nightmare from days earlier, reopening the sticky-sweet scabs that hadn't quite formed scars. The little girl had hair cemented by dried blood to the side of her head. Most of her cheek was chewed off and her eye dangled loose from its socket. Her skin was scraped and clawed, her lips were frayed and hung in slivers. Her head hung to the side and her arm remained rigid to the side while the other arched halfway up, her mangled fingers in a pose that seemed to be showing off a ring finger far too young to adorn one.

Her leg bent inward and her foot twisted on its side. She walked more on her ankle than her foot, which caused her stagger to be that much more prevalent. Then a gunshot to her head sent her falling backward into the legs of another dead thing moving forward, causing it to stumble on top of the little dead girl. That shook Janice from her thoughts, and she moved closer to her sons, reaching out for Joseph's arm.

Joseph turned around with fierce eyes that softened once he saw his mother.

"What are you doing? Why aren't you in the car?" Joseph asked.

"The car's been wrecked." She pointed back towards it.

"Fuck…are you okay? Are you hurt?"

"I'm fine, but we don't have a car. The Sheriff is telling everyone to leave…" she tried to yell over the noise.

"We can't just leave. We have to fight them."

"There's too many, honey. Let's go before it's too late…please," she coaxed him.

Eddie turned to see where his brother had gone, and noticed him and his mother talking.

"What's going on?" he asked.

"Car's fucked, that stupid cop crashed into it," his brother replied.

"Shit, let's back it up then, give us some more room." He began moving closer to the wall of the hall. "Guys," he yelled out, "move back!" But nobody could hear him. "Guys! Move back," he yelled as loud as he could, instantly getting hoarse.

They finally heard him and acknowledged by moving back. Once back, Eddie noticed Davis out of the corner of his eye. He was walking up to the deaders with an outstretched arm and shooting the creatures at close range, much like Sal had done with an empty gun.

"Oh, shit, he's lost it. Look at him," Eddie pointed out.

"Can't blame him, looks like its working though," Frankie replied. And with that he ran to Davis, shotgun in hand and backed him up.

"Frankie, don't be stupid," Eddie called out. But it was too late: by the time the words came out he was halfway there.

"Where are we going?" Dawn asked.

"I don't know! I don't fucking know!" Jon-Jon yelled, having lost any cool he once possessed.

"Don't yell at me," she said, her arm wrapped around Yussef.

"I'm sorry. I'm just scared shitless…I can't believe how many there are! It's like the gas station all over again..."

"I know...but don't take it out on me. We need to keep calm," she said, gesturing toward the small boy.

"Calm?" Jon-Jon laughed.

He pulled the van over to the side of the road and was haunted by the lyrics of one of his favorite songs: should I stay, or should I go? he thought, and heard the voice of Mick Jones reverberating in his head.

"If I stay...there will be double," he mumbled.

"What's that?" Dawn asked.

"Huh--? Oh, nothing, just thinking out loud."

"This is so fucked. I'm chicken shit for running out aren't I?"

"We're all scared," she said.

"Scared yeah, but I ran. In the end I'm just a bitch."

"We're alive, and that's how I want to stay."

"We're only alive because we've stuck together," Jon-Jon said, his tone shifting. "We're going back."

"Fine. Just don't get us killed," Dawn said, her eyes wet.

Scott had run out of ammunition and, after falling back with the rest of the line, he ran toward the tiny box he called a car. The blood streaked oversized Hot-Wheels sat crookedly down the slope on the front side of the VFW's grounds. It was only a few feet away, but every step felt like a mile away from Judy, and it pained him fiercely. He kept looking back, and then around, making sure to be on guard from all sides.

Scott took note of all the missing vehicles and quickly put the pieces together, or at least enough of them to make out the puzzle. He reached the car, got what he needed and hurried back while stuffing extra shells into his pockets. By the time he reached the line of defense he was reloading and catching his breath. Once he began firing, Frankie dropped back to do the same. Joseph clicked empty, and that was all he had. He tossed his empty gun toward the oncoming dead, but it fell short and hit the dirt.

"Come on, ma," he said, pulling her away from the line and toward the wrecked cars. He hoped there was something in the trunk with a few bullets left in it.

26 DEEPER DOWN

"So much for that damned wall," Walter slammed his fist on the windowsill.

"What's the matter, dad?" asked Barbara.

"Nothing good, sweetheart," he replied. He forced a smile on his tired face.

"Let me see," she said. She pushed past him to look out the window.

Pushing the curtain aside she looked out the window and gasped at what she saw. The dead things wandered through the fields to the rear of their home. They were spread apart, but numbered in the dozens with more even more in the distance.

"What are we going to do, dad?"

"Exactly what we planned on doing, sweetheart," he replied. "Now, calm down, take a deep breath. We're safe in here. Me and Jeff boarded the place up real tight. And if they do get in we can fight them off. This doesn't change anything, it was bound to happen so just keep your cool and stick to the plan."

Barbara didn't know what it was about her father that was so calming to her and she was in no mood to question it. She took a breath and found her resolve. Her father was right, they planned for this, they prepared for it, and now it was happening. She had things to do and now was the time to do them.

"I'll go tell mom and Jeff," she said.

He smiled at her. "Good girl, kiddo."

Once his daughter left the room and headed downstairs Walter turned his again-worried gaze to the dead things wandering around outside. Never planned for this many, he thought as he studied them. They're slow, he noticed, slow and unbalanced, but damn… there's so many.

"Dad." Jeff came running into the room. "What's going on?"

"Have a look-see," Walter said as he moved back from the window.

Jeff leaned over to look. "Shit," he said, "this is so crazy. It's one thing to see them on TV, but in real life…it makes you weak in the knees."

"Yeah, yeah it does. But we can't think about them. We got to think about ourselves."

Laura peeked in the room as Maria ushered the kids to their room.

"We have to keep our wits," Walter said. "We have to think ahead of them. We can't react, we have to act. Now, look at them. They're slow, and right now they're spread out. But if they get clumped together, slow or not we wouldn't stand a chance."

"Right, and if they all start pulling at the boards we'd be in for some trouble," Jeff said.

"It's early," Barbara noted. "That gives us plenty of daylight to be able to keep an eye on these things."

"And that's exactly what I want to do. I want to watch them, study them. I want to know everything about our enemy before we have to go toe to toe with them."

"Shouldn't we go for help?" Laura asked.

"No, Davis has been on top of things," Walter replied. "He either already has his hands full, or he's dead."

"Dead?" Laura asked, sounding shocked.

"Davis is the kind of guy that goes down with his ship. If these things are this close to us he already knows about them. If we go out looking for him we'd only be risking our lives even more. We're safe here for now, so that's exactly where we'll be staying."

No one argued, and no one wanted to go outside anytime soon.

***

Clem paced around the station. He'd gotten a solid couple hours of sleep, but his back ached, his neck was sore and his knees clicked with every step. He hated himself for getting so damned old and useless, but there wasn't anything he could do about it. He tried to walk the clicks out but they remained despite his efforts.

His stomach grumbled and he knew he could at least fix that. He walked around and eventually came across some packaged goods that would do the trick. He secretly hoped for a Pop-Tart but he didn't mind settling for the ass end of a sleeve of saltines.

He paced around some more, making his way to the windows at the front of the station. The street outside was deserted except for a few vehicles. No one was lingering around outside. A quiet morning, he thought, never thinking that would seem strange. But here it was and it just wasn't sitting right with him. Only a few hours ago it was as busy as a bus terminal in the city. Now, it wouldn't surprise him if tumbleweeds rolled by.

Danni was sleeping soundly, and after checking on her, Clem hoped he wouldn't make enough noise to wake her. Let the poor thing sleep, he thought. She needs it.

***

Jon-Jon drove back toward the VFW hall, avoiding several near accidents with the vehicles that were leaving the place.

"Maybe we shouldn't go back," Dawn said.

"If everyone's leaving we can just turn around again," he replied. "But if someone needs us then we're here."

"Okay. I was just sayin'."

"I know."

The van pulled up the hillside and sure enough the dead were still coming down. For all the fighting the living had done you would never notice. Most of the vehicles had pulled out and left. Jon-Jon could see the police cruiser had smashed into Eddie's car and neither would be able to drive out. He saw the vehicles were covered in blood and hoped to God that Eddie and his family were all right. He noticed the dozens of bodies strewn about and was relieved to see that none of them were fresh enough to be anyone he'd been surviving with—at least that's what he hoped.

"Over there!" Dawn pointed from the back.

"Oh, shit!" Jon-Jon said. "They're still going at it! Fuckers are crazy," he continued.

"Too crazy. Get them in here," she yelled.

Jon-Jon drove up fast, nearly startling the group that remained; Eddie, Joseph, Janice, Frankie, Scott, Judy, Chuck, and Chung-Hee. Before the van came to a stop Dawn opened the side door. "Get in," she yelled.

Chuck smiled. "Don't mind if I do," he said and wasted no time jumping in.

"It's now or never," Eddie said, rushing his mother inside.

Joseph called out to him. "Frankie, come on."

"We'll follow you," Judy said, leaving the group to run to her car, with Scott in tow.

"You got enough room or should I go with them?" Chung-Hee asked.

"Just get the fuck in," Jon-Jon said, eager to pull away from the approaching horde.

He did, and before they could close the door Jon-Jon spun around and sped away. Scott and Judy were already ahead of them.

27 DECISIONS

Dane was hurriedly packing his suitcase. He put two pairs of jeans in, a few shirts, socks and underwear. He grabbed a few photographs and an old watch that belonged to his grandfather. He looked around the room, his eyes locked onto the walkie-talkie, which had been silent for far too long, and he felt the pangs of guilt bite down hard.

Susan came back into the room with their toothbrushes and a bag full of toiletries. She threw them on the bed and then headed right for her closet. Dane snapped shut his suitcase satisfied with his selections.

"Okay, that's done," he said. "Now I'm going to go put whatever food and water I can into the truck."

"All right, go ahead. I'm almost done in here."

***

Davis ran out of ammunition and also ran out of rage. He jogged away from the oncoming horde and headed back to his truck, grabbing the ham radio.

"Where the fuck is everyone? Officer down! I repeat Officer down! The situation is out of control I need immediate back-up!"

The radio remained silent. He tried again to no avail and began to slam his fist on the steering wheel. He turned the ignition and sped away as fast as he could.

***

"Can't you get that thing to work, man?" Keith asked.

"I'm trying, but I can't do much without any tools," Topher replied.

"Fuck. I can't believe this is happening. It's like they all planned this. You know? Why are they in such a huge group?"

"I don't know, it doesn't make sense. They don't communicate with us, so could they communicate with each other? Is that possible?"

"Who knows? I just hope we can get to Bruce in time," Keith said, driving as fast as he could.

They zigzagged through the countless staggering dead that had come to town. They were everywhere. Some of the townspeople were outside fighting them with whatever they had. One man was fighting them off with a shovel, another with a garden rake. Others simply took to their cars and fled.

Where are they going? Keith wondered. The dead are everywhere.

"I think I was better off at the power station," Topher said, fumbling at his beard.

Keith tried to think of something reassuring to say to him, that he'd made the right decision. But he wasn't sure if even he agreed with the decision.

Two more minutes. Two more minutes and they'd be at the VFW hall. He just hoped that Davis could last that long.

***

Clem and Danni stared out the windows as the bloodied man approached the station. His hand clutched his throat which was bleeding terribly. His steps were tired and feet heavy, almost dragging on the pavement. In his right hand he held his service weapon at his side.

"Should we lock the door?" Clem asked.

"I think he's a cop," Danni replied. "I remember seeing him at the station yesterday. He's awful messed up, though…might not be safe. But what choice do we have?" Danni replied.

"I don't know. I don't know anything anymore. I guess if he turns, we can handle him, especially if it is just him. I don't see any body else coming."

"Guess you're right. If he turns, at least we can get his gun out of the deal," she said. She felt heartless even as the words left her mouth.

"Good thinking."

Clem went out the door, slowly approaching the man. "You need some help?"

The man nodded.

"Can you talk?" Clem asked.

"Yeah," the man said.

"What's you're name?"

"Jones," he replied.

"What happened, Jones?"

"Those things got me. They're everywhere."

"Shit. Let's get you inside."

Jones nodded, still clutching his bleeding wound.

Clem walked him inside as Danni held the door open. They sat Jones down. Danni rushed to get some wet paper towels while Clem looked for something to act as a bandage. Jones got up and walked over to the ham radio. It was turned off. He flipped it back on and grabbed the handset.

"The roadblocks are compromised…zombies everywhere…" he managed.

"Jones? Is that you? This is Davis…where the hell are you?"

"Yeah, it's Jones. I'm at the station…don't come here…fading fast, man…those things will be here too, soon enough."

"God damn it! Sal's gone. You're hurt, I haven't heard from anyone else…was anyone with you?"

"Yea…all dead…haven't seen Dane, or Keith though."

Danni came back with a bunch of wet paper towels and began to clean up his wounds. She touched him gently, but he winced regardless. Clem came back with a gauze pad and some duct tape.

"Best I could find," Clem said.

"Good enough," Jones replied. He didn't care one way or the other: he knew his time was short.

"Jones…how many deaders do you think you came across?" Davis asked.

"Over a hundred easy."

Driving as fast as he could, Davis kicked himself. Damn, we really are being overrun, he thought to himself. He was heading to the station, despite his inclination and warning from Jones.

***

"We're all packed up, let's get the hell out of here," Dane said.

Susan nodded as she grabbed the last bag of belongings and pulling Cher on her leash. She barked excitedly, thinking they were going out for a walk. She took one last look around. Her heart hurt at the thought of never setting foot into her home again, but she knew it would hurt more if she stayed.

She'd gotten this far in life by trusting her feelings, and though many might say it wasn't far at all, she couldn't be happier with how her life had turned out. Sure, there were things in her life she could have done without, the dead coming back for one, but she was healthy and loved and that was all she needed.

She looked to Dane and their eyes met and spoke what their mouths couldn't. She nodded, and left the room, looking back quickly once more.

Upon getting to the car Susan noticed the dead in the distance. Cher barked wildly, puffing up her chest as if to intimidate the dead. They were shambling about, some were moving closer to them while others were moving toward the other end of the street. Could they see her? She wondered, shivering at the thought. She tossed her bag in and followed right behind it. Dane closed the door and drove off.

"They're all over town, now. What do you think is happening, Dane?"

"I think we're leaving and it doesn't fucking matter, okay?"

"You don't have to be like that," she said as she stared out the window.

"No, I don't, you're right, but... I just feel like we're damned if we go and we're damned if we stay. We might not be any better off if we leave."

"I know, but trust me, it'll be worse if we stay. You know how you're knee hurts when it's about to rain?"

"Yeah..."

"Well, it's kinda like that, but picture the dead as rain."

"Yeah, but my knee feels fine."

"I'm not talking about your knee--I'm talking about me!"

"Do you ever make sense?" Dane smiled.

"Shut up--Oh, God, Dane look out!"

A little dead boy shuffled into the street. His shoe was on crooked, just barely on at all, and his shirt was covered in filth. Flies swirled around him with no fear of being swatted away. Dane almost ran him over, and he wouldn't have minded. But Susan's reaction caused him to slam on the brakes.

She wasn't as used to seeing the dead up close. She had stayed inside most of the time since it all began. They were still new to her and she stared at the boy with wet eyes, a quivering lip, and a newly found pity for the dead.

The dead boy staggered closer, reaching his hands toward the window. His stubby ripped fingertips streaked the glass as Susan stared into the boy's eyes. They were void of emotion, but the dark bags under them spoke of a bitter sadness. Dane reached for her hand as the wheels of the car began to roll again. Cher growled at the little boy, ready to pounce through the window if she had to.

***

"Where the fuck did everyone else go?" Eddie asked.

"Wish I knew, man," Jon-Jon replied. "People just left...and to tell you the truth we did too."

"Well, at least you came back for us," Joseph said, grateful that they had come back.

"So, what, everyone just scattered? They just took off just like that?" Eddie said, growing angry and hurt.

"Like I said...wish I knew," Jon-Jon said, keeping his eyes on the few vehicles they were following.

"Hey, uh...kid. Sorry, I forgot your name..." Joseph started.

"Yu-Yussef," the boy said, but could barely be heard.

"Right, Yussef, did you see what happened to Alexis?"

Yussef shook his head, keeping his eyes to the ground. Dawn looked apologetically at Joseph, knowing he cared for her and not knowing what to say to him. She wanted to tell him that she was okay, and that they would all meet up again soon, but she couldn't do that. She knew that there was a very good possibility she was dead. She finally managed to say, "I didn't see her, Joe. It was so crazy, everyone was running around like lunatics...getting into whatever car they could and taking off."

He nodded. Joseph couldn't see Alexis just taking off, though. Especially leaving behind one of the kids. She could have been extremely flustered and not have counted them, assuming they had all followed her and maybe even now she was looking for the lost little boy. He doubted it, but wondered nonetheless where and how she was.

He wouldn't admit it openly, but he could feel her absence in his gut. He'd grown to like her a lot over the past few days, which was unusual for Joseph. He was a young guy who never cared much for the attachment of a girlfriend, but in a world overrun by the dead he was beginning to see the upside to having one, and he really wanted one. But as luck would have it she was nowhere to be found. The grief he felt for his father and siblings had to be playing a role in his emotional attachment as well.

***

Alexis sat in the backseat of an SUV. She didn't really know the folks she was driving with well, but remembered their names. Abdul-Ba'ith was driving the vehicle. Next to him in the passenger seat was the constantly hysterical chubby woman who Alexis thought was named Carrie, but couldn't recall. She was getting on everyone's nerves and only adding to the children's growing anxiety.

Alexis sat in the back with most of the children she had taken care of in Gerty's absence, and now missed her even more. She thought that if Gerty was still around she wouldn't have lost one of the kids in all the commotion. She hated herself for leaving, but couldn't risk the lives of the rest of them for the sake of one. She could've stayed and left the kids alone with the folks from the gas station, but she didn't know them well enough and after being in the truck with them for the last few minutes she knew Carrie would be useless and Abdul would have his hands full. He was quiet, and seemed put together. But could she trust this man who looked like a terrorist to take these kids to safety? She couldn't make that decision. She had to have faith that someone else from her group would have taken Yussef to safety. She had to. She had to have hope and faith, otherwise she didn't see the point in trying to survive.

She held Leela in her lap with her arm around Chris, patting his head as they cried gently. Nick and Stacey cried as well, but their eyes were glued to the rear window.

"Where are we going?" Alexis asked.

"I don't know," Abdul-Ba'ith replied, looking at her in the rearview mirror. "I'm just following the cars ahead."

"I'm not sure any of them no where to go. We all just took off right? Did you hear anybody say anything?" She asked.

"No. No one said anything, they just took off, I just figure they didn't want to tell me," Abdul-Ba'ith replied.

"Oh," she said, unsure of what to say next. "There's no one behind us and I don't see any of those things around," she said. "Maybe we should pull over and wait to see if anyone else has come this way?"

"Sure, that sounds good," he replied.

"What? No!" Carrie screamed. "Let's follow the others, lets stick with them!"

"Please relax," Abdul-Ba'ith said, "they're just driving blind: they have no plan."

"That doesn't mean we should stop on the side of the road and lose the only other people we know," she cried.

"We don't know any of those people," he said, pulling over to the side of the road.

"Others will come this way," Alexis spoke softly. "You'll see. The ones who stayed to fight. The ones who have a real plan, not the ones who were quick to leave."

"This is bullshit!" Carrie yelled, crossing her arms.

"Bullshit or not. We're waiting," Abdul-Ba'ith glared at her, his patience almost at an end.

***

Davis saw a car approaching in the distance. It was a police cruiser and it was speeding forward. Davis slowed down and the other car did the same as they neared each other.

"Bruce!" Keith yelled, as he got out of the cruiser.

"Holy shit am I glad to see you," Davis replied.

Topher got out as well but stayed behind the door, his head spinning around to keep an eye out for any zombies.

"Talk to me," Davis said.

"These fucks are all over town, man. It's like they just appeared out of nowhere. We were digging near the roadblock, right, and then they were on the road, coming out of the hills. Then I heard Jones on the radio. He had them everywhere as well. So we tried to kill some of them off and, before we knew it, they were getting close and we were running out of ammo. My radio's all fucked up, the cruiser's just about shot to shit, and now we're here."

"That was a mouthful. So you weren't with Jones?"

"No. Haven't heard from him either, have you?"

"Yeah...he's at the station. He's...been bitten, and everyone he was with is dead."

"No...oh, fuck, man. What the fuck..." Keith rubbed his neck.

"I know, I know. I'm heading over there now, you two want to hop in and join me?"

"What else would we do?"

"Good, get whatever you have and jump in."

***

"Look, there's a truck pulled over. Slow down," Judy pointed out.

"I am, I am," Scott hushed her, pulling over.

Jon-Jon and the others watched as Scott and Judy pulled up alongside the truck. Eddie and the others tried to look from the back seat. No one recognized the truck. Jon-Jon slowly approached the truck, and before he could figure out who it was Abdul-Ba'ith hopped out of the drivers seat and raised a friendly hand in the air. Carrie followed him, and so did Alexis after she told the kids to stay put.

Dawn got out of the van and ran over to her. They hugged tightly and began to cry.

"Oh, God, you're okay. We were so worried," Dawn said.

"Me too, did you happen to see where--"

"We got Yussef," she cut her off before she could finish.

"Oh, Thank God! I couldn't find him and they were going to leave...I had to get the others out of there," Alexis started.

"Shh. Come on," Dawn said.

Joseph opened the side of the van and got out. He smiled at her and she smiled back. "I thought I'd never see you again," he said.

"You're not getting away that easy," she said, hugging him closely. Then making her way into the van to hug Yussef. "Sweetheart, I'm so sorry I lost you! Are you okay?"

He nodded shyly, as if he'd done something wrong. Alexis lifted his head up with her hands, forcing him to make eye contact with her red, crying eyes. "I'm so sorry."

He couldn't look away and mumbled, "it's okay."

She hugged him again, tight enough to hurt, but he smiled at the squeeze.

"What's the plan?" Abdul-Ba'ith asked.

"Not really sure, man," Scott said, "I guess it's just us that's left. You know where the others went?"

"No, they just kept going," Abdul-Ba'ith replied.

"Well, fuck them then." Scott was surprised by his own harshness. "Don't have a plan--they seem to be useless anyway."

"True," he nodded in agreement.

Jon-Jon and Eddie joined them in the middle of the road. "What are we doing?"

"That's what we were just trying to figure out. Any ideas?" Scott asked.

"Yeah I got a few... I think we should head north. Get as far as we can. I think if we can make it to colder climates we can let the weather take care of the dead and we just worry about staying alive. My other idea is just to keep moving." He pointed at a group of lurkers that were staggering through the brush just past the side of the road. "It looks like we got company."

"That sounds good, but how the hell are we supposed to get north?" Scott said. "The roads are shit, you know that."

"I know, but that doesn't mean we can't try. What are our other options? We can't go back. We sure as hell can't kill them all, they've already overrun the town," Jon-Jon said, trying to make his point.

"I say we start heading northeast," Eddie added. "Much of the shore towns should be pretty empty now. We can just follow the coast up and hope for a blizzard."

"A bit too early for a blizzard," Abdul-Ba'ith said.

The dead had found their way to the road. A woman in a nightgown staggered into view. Her left breast was dangling out of her gown and looked like shredded beef. The entire left side of her body looked like it had been bitten and scratched repeatedly by a large beast. Her mouth mashed the air and a gurgling noise crawled out of her throat.

"Time to go. Are we agreed?" Jon-Jon asked.

"Sure."

"Why Not?"

"Let's go."

***

Walter returned to the window. He stared out at the dead. The bodies of the ones he and Jeff just dispatched remained motionless. They beat them down with shovels and ran back inside. Walter was still high on adrenaline, but he had to remain calm. He took several deep breaths and tried to relax but he was too wired now. He felt like he'd drank an entire pot of coffee. His hands shook and he couldn't make them stop. His hands had a mind of their own now.

"So we're staying?" Barbara asked, Maria standing at her side.

"Yep. I think its best. We don't know what the rest of the town is like. We could be running from the heat and into the fire," he told them.

"Okay," she said.

"That okay with you?" Jeff asked Maria as he returned from the bathroom, rubbing his stomach.

"Whatever you think is safest. I don't want to take the kids out there unless we have to," she said as she rubbed Jeff's arm.

"Me too."

Laura sat with the kids and watched them play, oblivious to the dead outside. She could almost overhear the conversation in the other room. She knew the kids weren't paying attention otherwise she would have gone in there and shushed them.

"There's more coming," Walter said. "Look, over there," he pointed out.

"Damn," Jeff said. "I wonder how many are out there?"

"Probably a lot more than we think," Walter replied, "so long as we stay on top of them we'll be all right," he hoped.

28 SINKING SHIP

As Davis approached the station he had to weave in and out of the dead that wandered the streets of his once quiet little town. He turned down the street and saw the station with a group of maybe seven or so of the deaders trying to get in the front door.

"Bastards," he grumbled.

"You want to pull up and I'll shoot them?" Keith asked.

"Yeah, guess so."

Davis pulled up, trying to avoid the shambling dead that walked toward them. His truck had taken a bad enough beating as it was and he'd like it to remain drivable. Once they were close enough Keith began to pick them off. They never turned to see why their brethren were falling down dead. All they seemed to care about was getting inside the doors. Keith took out the last one and they headed for the doors.

The doors were locked, but looking out at them was a younger woman with haunted eyes. When she realized that Davis, Keith, and Topher were not flesh-eating zombies she unlocked the door and let them in.

"Where's Jones?" Davis barked.

"He's in there," Danni said as she pointed to the room where she'd left him.

They rushed past her and moved toward Jones. She locked the door again, staring out through the blood streaked glass. Clem greeted them with a grim expression that said hello and sorry at the same time. He moved out of the way and joined Danni by the door.

"Jones," Davis mumbled.

"Hey...guys," he coughed, revealing a smile full of bloody teeth.

"Shit, man... I can't believe this is happening," Keith said as he looked at his friend, already mourning him.

"Me neither...we still going...fishing this weekend right?" Jones asked.

"Yeah, man, definitely..." Keith began to sob.

"You better be able to get your ass up early, though," Davis joined in. "None of that nine o'clock bullshit."

"You got it..." Jones eyes rolled up into the back his head.

"Oh, no..." Keith whimpered, "Is he...?"

"I think so." Davis's eyes welled up.

Jones didn't move. His chest didn't rise and fall, and when he opened his eyes again their friend was nowhere to be found in them. The dead Jones moved fast, lurching toward them. He grabbed Keith's arm but he was able to pull it away before Jones could bite it. Davis put two in his head. Blood spattered all over the HAM radio behind him. Topher walked away, heading toward Danni and Clem. He introduced himself as Keith and Davis let their emotions get the better of them.

"I think we got trouble," Danni said. "There's a lot of them coming up."

"Yeah, shit. More and more keep coming into the street," Clem noted.

"I should've never left," Topher mumbled.

"What's that?" Clem asked.

"Nothing."

Clem continued to stare out the window. The dead, in all their sickening varieties, stumbled forward. Some walked on broken legs, others crawled on the pavement pulling behind a trail of intestines, some walked with a hitch or a twitch and others seemed to walk as well as the living.

"Hey, Sheriff, I hate to bother you right now, but we got plenty of company coming up the street."

"Let me see," he said as he made his way to the door.

He looked, and he didn't like what he had seen. His expression grew grim and his eyes narrowed. "Keith," he said as he turned toward the man, "let's get to the armory."

Keith nodded, wiping away a trail of tears from his cheek.

"You two stay here and make sure they don't get inside. We'll be back in a minute. I hope you two can shoot."

By the time they returned from the armory the dead had swarmed the front doors. They clawed and bit and struck the glass. Danni and Clem had retreated to the second set of double-doors and locked it as well, peering through the much smaller windows in the centers of the doors.

"Fuck, they got here quick." Davis dumped his armful of weapons on the nearest desk. The others did the same.

They all took up arms. Davis quickly showed Clem and Danni what to do with what they had picked up. They opened the set of double-doors and began firing through glass entry doors. The sounds of the multiple weapons firing was intense. Glass shattered to the floor as the bullets pierced through finding their intended targets. Their ears rang from the firing and quickly felt cotton-filled.

Despite the proximity to the dead, the number of headshots were small. Most of the bullets hit dead flesh, but not hard enough to push them back. The few that were shot in the head dropped to the ground, but the others moved forward without the obstacle of the glass doors.

Davis quickly took aim and dispatched as many as he could while Keith reloaded and helped the others do the same. The dead were able to close the distance from the entryway doors to the doors the living fought to protect. The plan was to kill them all and flee in his truck. The plan failed…miserably.

Behind the dead were more dead, and behind those were even more. Though they had the weapons for the job, they didn't have the personnel.

"Get inside," Davis yelled.

"Shit. They're getting through!" Keith yelled.

They continued firing. More dropped, but plenty more were there to fill the void. They couldn't keep them back. They were pushing through the door as Davis and the others fought to close them.

"God damn it! Fall back!" Davis screamed.

They fell back to the first row of desks, and continued to shoot the oncoming dead. They flooded in. The dead that led the way acted as shields for the numbers behind them and before long they were in the station and forcing the living to continue moving back. They grabbed what extra guns they could, but it quickly ceased to matter.

"Get to the back!" Davis yelled, as he ran to lead the way.

Once at the rear of the station the front filled in quickly. Davis looked out the window in the back and saw that the building was surrounded. There was no way out. They sacrificed their chance of getting downstairs, as well as the roof, by running to the back of the building. Now they had only three choices: suicide, do nothing and let the dead feast on them, or lock themselves into one of the holding cells.

They ran inside the cell, barely having time to do anything else. Davis slammed the door shut and heard the clink of the lock. They sat against the wall as the dead hands reached in between the cold cell bars. They grasped at the air. Their retched lifeless growls and grunts bounced off the cool brick wall and nested inside the cotton-filled ears of the prisoners.

Danni stood up, lining the barrel of her gun up with one of the deader's heads. His nose looked like small lumpy potato and his face like burnt cheese. She pulled the trigger. Her ears filled with still more cotton. The dead man fell slumped to the ground, the contents of his head spilling onto the floor.

"Save your bullets," Davis suggested, "we might just need them for ourselves."

They watched the blood slowly pool around the dead man's body, amazed at how much blood was left.

29 AND HELL FOLLOWED WITH

Jon-Jon led the way out of New Haven, with Scott and Judy in tow, and Abdul behind them. The convoy was smaller now, all the hangers-on had left in a hurry. They weren't missed and considering their new plan of action it may have ultimately been for the better. The trek north would certainly be a challenge, but if Jon-Jon was right with his assumptions the dead wouldn't be able to fair the weather as well as the living. He just hoped he was right and not risking everyone's lives for a pipe dream.

On their way out of town they past the 'You are now leaving New Haven, Come again soon!' sign and the half-dug ditches by the side of the road. The bodies of the dead had become nothing more than part of the worlds new nightmarish landscape, and as commonplace as road signs.

Alexis told the kids not to look at the bodies, but they didn't seem to be bothered by them anymore. In the short time since the world came to an end they had all grown desensitized and callous, perhaps a necessity to survive. Alexis wondered what the coming days would bring and shuddered at the possibilities. They were all bleak, but she had hope and she had a purpose; she had the kids, and they were all reunited again. And she and her friends had each other. She supposed she'd get to know Abdul and Carrie, though she seemed more trouble than she was worth. But maybe she would snap out of it?

Maybe...

"Next stop--Disney Land!" Jon-Jon kidded.

Dawn looked at him in that what-the-hell-is-wrong-with-you kind of way, which immediately obliterated the goofy smirk he had on his face. He looked embarrassed and decided to keep his eyes on the road and his mind on driving.

Chung-Hee closed his eyes and hoped to find sleep. But all he saw was the red face of Yama, the god of the dead. Chung-Hee grew up listening to his family speak of the God Generals, ancient deities, and the all the different hells he could go to if he ever misbehaved. His youthful arrogance and dismissal of his family's beliefs now had him questioning his own and wondering if this was his punishment for his ignoble actions in life. And he wondered if this was in fact one of the hells his parents cautioned him of.

He couldn't think of anything he had ever done that could bring about such wrath, but maybe his place in a world that held commerce and science above faith and devotion was enough. Maybe Yama saw fit to purge the Earth with a plague of the dead and transform it into Naraka. He had no reason to believe that was a possibility, but in light of recent times anything had become possible.

Eventually he found sleep.

Eddie and Joseph looked at each other. They didn't need words anymore to communicate, it was like they could read each other's minds now.

"You want to do this?" Eddie asked anyway.

"I don't know what I want to do, it all seems hopeless, man."

Dawn turned toward the back and listened. She didn't want everyone to start getting down, knowing all too well what that would do to their momentum.

"Sometimes, yeah, but all the hope I need is you and ma and everyone else in this van. All we have to do is outlast those things and we'll be fine. They're dead and decaying, and all we have to do is stay alive long enough for them to fall apart, right?"

"I guess...if we don't get killed before then."

"We won't. Not if we stick together like we've been doing."

"He's right, dude," Chuck chimed in. "When I was at the airport it was chaos. Everyone was out for themselves and I barely got out of there because of it. If we all stick together we can make it up north and just ride it out."

"I hope so, I really do," Joseph said.

Eddie was pained by his brother's continually declining shift in mood. They had been through a lot and he didn't know what to say anymore. He was never much for brotherly advice, and rarely had any to give. But he had to say something.

"We just have to keep going. No matter what, we can't give up. If we give up now it's like everyone we loved died for nothing. We have to honor their memories by staying alive."

Janice sat quietly, tears running down her face. She was proud of her boys--proud of her men. As much as she wanted to give up and go out with the tide they kept her anchored at shore.

"How much gas do we have?" Frankie asked.

"Not enough," Jon-Jon replied. "About half a tank."

"Great. Wake me up when we have to start walking," Frankie said and closed his eyes.

Scott turned on the radio, more out of habit than anything else, and couldn't believe it when he heard voices through the speakers.

...continue repeating this Emergency Alert System broadcast until we have new information.

The message was then followed by a two-toned sound similar to the Emergency Broadcast sounds used in television. Scott and Judy listened impatiently for the message to repeat. Scott sped up alongside the van. He rolled down his window and yelled for them to turn on the radio, then he dropped back and did the same for Abdul. The two-toned sound started again, lasting about twenty-seconds and then the broadcast started.

This is an Emergency Alert System broadcast originating from the Mount Weather Special Facility in West Virginia.

There is a worldwide phenomenon occurring where clinically dead humans are reanimating and attacking living humans in an attempt to eat living flesh. Early attempts at dispatching the reanimated hostiles, destroying the brain, seemed effective. However, new evidence suggests we now warn that this is insufficient. Specimens assumed dead continue to reanimate. There is no consistent timeframe for which a hostile will reanimate. The only permanent way of dispatching the hostiles is by incineration, or the use of a chemical agent to dissolve the remains.

It is also safest to stay off the roads and out of heavily populated areas. If you have found a safe haven it is recommended you remain there. Specially equipped units of the military are in the process of reclaiming key strategic areas around the nation. Once we are able to reclaim those areas we will reinstate the Emergency Transportation System to aid survivors in getting to those locations.

We will continue repeating this Emergency Alert System broadcast until we have new information.

***

Pulled over once more along the empty roads out of New Haven Jon-Jon, Abdul, Eddie, Judy and most of the others stood outside of their vehicles to discuss the broadcast. They heard it as it continued to play in a never-ending loop in the background.

"It doesn't change a thing," Scott insisted.

"I think he's right," Joseph added.

"But doesn't it make more sense for us to head down to Virginia?" Dawn disputed. "That's where the broadcast is coming from."

"It makes sense, but why haven't we heard anything from the government till now, weeks later?" Eddie asked. "I don't trust that they can help us, we've stayed alive this far without them…"

Alexis jumped in. "Yeah, but they must be doing something right if they're taking over certain areas. Areas that we can try to get to!"

"It's been weeks! WEEKS! And, now we're supposed to go to Virginia in the hopes that our lousy government can finally do something for us?" Scott grew angered.

"Not to say anything bad about our great nation, but it took them over a month to stop an oil spill. I think we are better off taking care of ourselves," Abdul added sheepishly.

"Yeah, he's right man!" Chuck said. "My cousin was volunteering to clean off sea turtles and ducks and shit while the politicians were busy pointing fingers as the shit got worse. And this ain't an oil spill we're dealing with--"

A gunshot broke through the night and a bullet entered a deader's head, erupted out of the back of it and pulled with it chunks of brain, bone, skin, and hair. Carrie walked in front of the truck and fired another shot. She missed the other dead thing but fired again and the creature dropped. "There's more. We need to make a decision."

"Shall we take a vote?" Jon-Jon asked.

"Fuck it, why not?" Frankie asked.

North it was.

30 CURIOSITY

West Virginia.
Mount Weather Special Facility.

Rachel Lucas and Doctor Gregory Tran put in a request to work together. They had to justify the request with their superiors and upon furnishing their findings they had gotten what they wanted. With a catch, of course.

A young soldier sat restrained on the examination table usually reserved for the dead. He was a blond haired kid from Texas not even old enough to drink. He was sedated but his eyes were penetrating and gut-wrenching regardless. After hearing what the catch was Rachel tried everything she could to stop it from happening, but failed. When she was given the choice to take the soldier's place she decided to keep her own. As a result she couldn't look the kid in the eyes.

The kid soldier was hooked up to a mechanical respirator in the hopes that once given a lethal injection his brain would still be getting oxygen. In theory it would present Rachel and Tran with the best possible specimen in which to continue their research. They also had a medical infusion pump and a dialysis machine in the corner of the room should they decide to use them.

Several guards stood outside of the room accompanied by the Deputy Secretary of Defense, William T. Pymn II, who nodded for Tran to carry out the lethal injection. Tran grimly nodded back. He too didn't want to sacrifice a soldier of all people, but figured it was better than the alternative.

He administered the injection and the young man tried to squirm but was too heavily restrained to move. Tran and Rachel watched the monitors as the young man died before them. His heart stopped first and then all brain activity ceased. The mechanical respirator kept him breathing as planned.

His eyes opened even though clinically he was dead. He had no pulse, no heartbeat, and no brain activity. Yet he could speak.

"Brains," the thing muttered. "Flesh," as his jaw moved and his eyes flitted around the room.

"What is your name?" Tran asked.

"Death."

END

ABOUT THE AUTHOR

Steve Wands lives in New Jersey with his wife and son. He's a freelance artist by day and writer by night. He drinks too much coffee, and sleeps very little. He is the author of the *Stay Dead* series of short stories, collections, and novels as well as *Horror Stories: A Macabre Collection, Words Like Daggers, Modern Nightmares,* and plenty of short stories. He also co-edited and contributed to *Dark: A Horror Anthology.*

You can visit his blog here: http://www.stevewands.blogspot.com or play with his twitter: http://twitter.com/swands

If Google Groups are your thing, than why not join Steve's: http://groups.google.com/group/apparatus-revolution